Soul Mirror

Edmund Stone

Published by Crystal Lake Publishing
Where Stories Come Alive!

Crystal Lake Publishing
www.CrystalLakePub.com

WELCOME
TO ANOTHER

CRYSTAL LAKE PUBLISHING
CREATION

Join today at www.crystallakepub.com & www.patreon.com/CLP

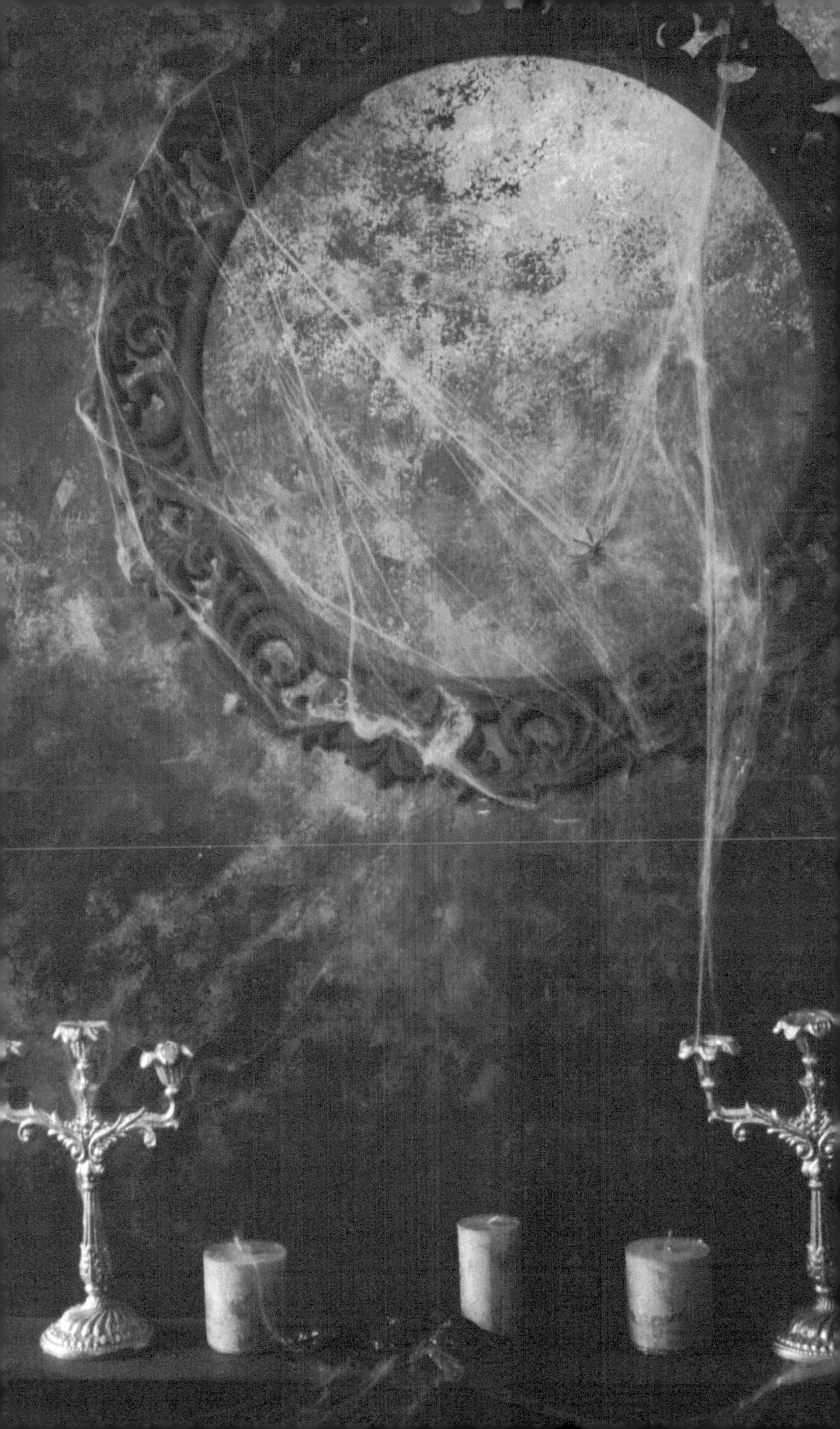

To Mikel, my love and reason for every day
To Laynie, Carver, Ellie, Beau, and Boone
Never stop dreaming
To all the therapy kids who touched my life, this one's for you

FOREWORD

As a grateful participant in the indie horror literature community (because that's exactly what it is, a community), I spend most of my free time with delightful weirdos. A good number of those weirdos are fellow authors. Over the past few years, I've met dozens of them and consider every single one to be a friend, and these friendships tend to be about much more than books. I read their words daily, chat with them online as often as possible, exchange inside jokes, meet their loved ones, and make plans in advance of those rare occasions where we are able to hang out in person. It's become a huge part of my life, this circle of delightful weirdos; a safe space, a second (and chosen) family. And it's a large group, growing larger all the time.

But even as that circle widens and deepens around me, Edmund Stone continues to stand out. He was one of the very first of these weirdos I met, along with his lovely wife Mikel, and remains one of my closest friends in the community. We partner on events and writing projects, share successes and ask each other questions and favors constantly. When he asked me to write an intro for Soul Mirror, I was honored. My first thought was to talk about how I think this is his best work yet (which is my honest, hand-to-heart sentiment about it, you see), but I also want to help you understand why that is, dear reader. Because it's more than just something I'm saying. It's something I believe.

So, why is this book special?

Edmund Stone is a writer's writer, you should hear that first. He has this enviable versatility, combined with an imagination that runs like a waterfall. These qualities make a difference, and not every person who writes a book has them. I've read stories he's written about ancient entities that breed armies in a small town and fill the air with floating body parts, or about secret covens of witches that use their bizarre powers to pursue hidden agendas, or about blood-soaked rampages achieved through the use of a machete empowered by the devil himself, or even about radioactive snowfall that turns people into zombies with a dash of taxidermy thrown in for good measure. Plus, he can make these stories oscillate between violence, chilling imagery, believable character actions, a quietly unsettling atmosphere, or a full-bore shot of terror, all within a handful of pages. It's enough to make me wonder if there's anything he *can't* write about.

Enter Jessica and her Soul Mirror...

I say again, I've gotten to know a lot of writers, and have grown fond of them all. But if I had to pick one who is up to the task of writing a full novel from the point of view of a troubled and neurodivergent child, it would be Edmund. Because of everything I described above, and also because I know how much of his life has been dedicated to helping kids just like that. It's a unique perspective, that few adults can assimilate and few writers can tackle, and now you get to share in the experience as he pulls it off with grace. You'll travel with Jessica and her supporting cast as she sees herself pulled into a through-the-looking-glass scenario full of wonder, impossible choices, supernatural happenings, and steep consequences. This story is compelling, it's tense, it's mysterious, and as you're likely hoping, it's fucking scary.

I'll close with a few words of advice...

Stick close to Jessica, she's got a better chance of surviving than we do and things are not as they seem where we're going. Watch your back around that upside-down house, and be wary of any voices you hear inside the mirror. Oh, and expect a few surprises along the way.

Ben Young
November, 2024

PART ONE
Soul Mirror

One
The Mirror

Jessica's world is upside down. Her life is an amalgamation of reality and dreams, as tangible to the mind as it is to the touch. Inside the mirror, she finds a place where she can escape the confines of the real world. Her body causes her pain and discomfort, affecting her ability to speak out there. The doctors call it Autism and it makes it frustratingly hard to cope. In here though, it all goes away.

She screams at the top of her lungs and listens to the echoes of her voice in the distance. This is her second time here and so far, the longest stint yet. Jessica typically wakes in her bed afterward, making the whole thing seem like an illusion. But it feels so real and she wants to stay.

On this trip, a house looms ahead with a juxtaposition that shouldn't be possible. The roof points to the foundation, which houses normally rest on. Little stones line the side of the house and they speak to her with the playful voices of children. They say, *go inside, play with us. You'll have fun.*

Jessica has no friends, so the thought of children wanting to play with her is exciting. This is something she never feels like most other emotions she tries to regulate in the real world. It's a wonderful feeling and she's drawn there, but before she can step on the porch, she hears someone calling. Yellow eyes stare back in the distance, permeating the darkness, mesmerizing her. But before disseminating their meaning, she's pulled backward and away from where she is. She closes her eyes. When she opens them, she's back in her room.

"Jessica! Wake up, girl, before he gets in here! Move your ass!" her mother says, "And I don't want excuses either."

Jessica rolls from the bed and sits on the edge for a moment. Her mother paces in front of her in only a bra and panties. Her skin is tight around her ribs, and Jessica thinks she can count all of them. Things like this fascinate her and if the woman would stand still long enough, she could immerse herself in the task, but her mother won't, and she knows this. A cigarette dangles in the woman's hand, and she brings it to her mouth and takes a long dramatic draw. She releases the smoke and as it rolls around her head, she yells again.

"Get up and get going. You don't want your dad coming in here," she says, then turns for the door. Her mother slams it open, letting it hit the wall, producing a thump that brings Jessica to attention. She wishes she could protest, scream at the top of her lungs to make her mother listen, but she can't. She has never been able to form anything more than grunts that fall on deaf ears.

Her hands make contact with the dirty mattress and her skin crawls. It felt like tiny worms were invading her body, entering through her fingertips. She sees the mirror across the room, reflecting a thirteen-year-old girl. But to her, it's the face of someone distorted and scary. Her hair is stringy and unwashed and her once-white pajamas are stained from the filth of the mattress and everything else in the house. She scratches at a spot on her arm.

Another mark left by the small bugs that inhabit her mattress. Even though the sensation of the bites drives her crazy, she's learned to live with it. Like so many other things in her life. Her inability to talk among them.

Her voice may not cooperate with her, but her hearing is excellent. Her parents, Wanda and Carl, or rather foster parents—the word she's heard multiple times, especially when they like to deride her—can't seem to understand this. They bellow loudly nearby, treating her as though she's not there and only a fixture in the room she inhabits.

In reality, Jessica's world is beyond repair, and she uses everything she has to make it worth living, even the things not always afforded her. The mirror, for example, gives her an escape from this gloomy place. She's vanished in there before, always getting to the house but never inside.

The first time was by accident and happened only weeks ago. Ever since then, the mirror invades her dreams during her waking and sleeping consciousness. And every time the children call for her.

Her parents yell outside her door. Their voices echo in the small house, sending shock waves through her nerve endings. She can hear them as though they were next to her.

"Why ain't you ready yet? We got to get that fucking kid in there to the therapy clinic across town and we're already late," Carl says to Wanda. "What is on your face?"

Jessica stands and walks nearer the door where she can see them bickering. She peeks out the door, staring at them, watching as Wanda turns her head from Carl.

"It's dirt I suppose. It just showed up there," Wanda says.

"Well, get it cleaned up. We got a lot to do today. She needs to get to therapy before Child Protective Services starts knocking at our door."

Jessica sinks back into the room, closing the door gently when Carl looks her way.

He's watching her in the way he does. Dark shadows cover his face. All she sees are his eyes. She shivers and goes to her chest of drawers to find some clothes. The bottom drawer is open and spilling on the floor, broken like everything else in this place. She rifles through the things and finds a worn and dirty hoodie with a logo of the Cincinnati Bengals pasted on the front.

Jessica takes off her pajama top and throws it into the corner. She puts on the fairly clean shirt and pulls it down over her body, adjusting it the best she can. The feel of it bothers her. It's tighter than before and she realizes why even though she doesn't understand it. Her body is changing. Things are getting bigger on her chest and she's becoming taller. The whole transformation has been sudden, and she wants someone to explain this to her, but can't find an adult to help. The confusion is enough to make her scream inside her head.

Lately, everything is a jumbled mess in there and it's only getting worse. She wants to smack her head, hit herself to wake up whatever animal is emerging within her.

When she goes to the upside-down world in the mirror, she becomes something outside of herself. A normal talking girl where children talk back to her.

She recalls the first time she heard them.

The chatter was incessant as they talked to her while she was in her bed. Late at night when the only thing in the house heard was the low laughing on the television in the front room. The place where Wanda and Carl sat and the bird squawked. The crazy animal she hates. The children called to her that night and she went to them. Ever since, the mirror has been a refuge. Jessica's hiding place from the real world.

The door swings open, slamming into the wall again. The noise causes Jessica to cringe.

Wanda walks in, clothed now, but her hair is disheveled, sticking up on the ends. She has a brush with her, and without warning, starts pulling crazily through the tangled mess on Jessica's head. Her movements are erratic, and she barks orders like a drill sergeant. She inspects Jessica with roaming eyes, then stops brushing for a moment.

"Why aren't you ready yet?" she says. "You can't go out with those pants on."

Wanda takes a step, more like a small leap, toward the closet. A light comes on, dull and yellow, like the once-white walls of the house. They are stained like most everything here. Wanda pulls her clothes back, the ones hung on the rail. Most are on the floor where they've been for a long time. Wanda rarely does laundry and when she does it's a big ordeal with lots of swearing. Those times are stressful for Jessica, like every other event her foster parents initiate. Jessica turns and stares at the mirror and wishes for it to take her away, but the only response she gets is the cold, expressionless stare of herself looking back at her. She hoped for a better response.

She feels something strike the back of her head, not hard, but enough to make her jump. A pair of worn jeans fall to the floor beside her. She doesn't pick them up, only looks at the lump of fabric like any other lifeless thing.

"What are you doing? Put those on and I'll be back to finish brushing your hair," Wanda says, walking out the door.

Jessica loathes having her hair brushed. It's like needles poking her all over her head.

She puts on the jeans, tugging and stretching the fabric. The button won't come together in front. The pants had gotten tighter around her hips. It didn't matter though, she had never been able to button her pants anyway. Her fingers won't come together correctly no matter how many times she tries. She gives up on the endeavor and instead crouches in front of the mirror, looking at her reflection. She tries to stare beyond it, to a place far inside, away from the chaos ensuing around her. She brings her hand in front of her face and lets it twitch there, side to side, from the back of her hand to the palm. This relaxes her and helps her focus on the mirror. Wanda will be back soon, and she wants to escape. But for the time being it looks as though it won't happen.

Two
The Clinic

Wanda storms into the room again, puffing away at the cigarette in her mouth. Ashes fall onto Jessica's arm, and she flinches, then bats at it wildly.

"Don't worry about that, it won't bite," Wanda says. "My momma burned me with a lit one when I got out of hand. Which, I can tell you was a bunch. I still have the scars."

She laughs in a raspy voice. "Here, quit looking at yourself in that mirror. You must be the vainest person I know. Always staring at yourself. Let me brush your hair and then you'll see a pretty girl staring back at you instead of the mess you are right now. Come over here to the bed where I can get a better hold on you."

Jessica complies, standing and walking to the bed. She sits, hearing the crush of the fabric on the mattress much better than Wanda. The feel of the thing has not improved, and it makes Jessica's unease grow. She sees the brush in Wanda's hand and her apprehension intensifies. Wanda pulls the plastic grill through Jessica's hair, and it hits resistance immediately. Jessica jumps away, shaking her head wildly, making sounds, but no words, and notices Wanda getting visibly angry with her.

"Hold still, Jessica," she says.

Jessica will have no part of it. She stands and goes back to the mirror, dropping to her knees then puts her hand in front of her face again and rocks back and forth. Her eyes dart around, looking for something inside.

Then she sees what she's looking for just beyond the edge of her reflection. The mirror bends there. A fraction of light stretching somewhere in the distance. Before she can concentrate on it though, she's taken away suddenly by a hand tugging on her arm.

Wanda forcefully makes her stand.

"Listen here, you little bitch. I'm running the show and Carl said to have you ready. Now get to your feet and let me finish your hair!"

Jessica whimpers inside but allows Wanda to do it even though it hurts. It doesn't help that Wanda's hands are so shaky she can't get an even brush stroke going. She wishes Wanda would go away and leave her alone, let her get lost in the mirror forever. Wanda finishes pulling her bald and then releases Jessica while she runs out of the room again.

More ashes fall onto Jessica's skin, and she rubs the area furiously.

Jessica starts for the mirror again when Carl enters. He has a phone in his hand and stares at her in a way she doesn't like. "Yes, that'll work," he says into the phone, "When the time's right, she'll be ready." He flips the device closed, then smiles at Jessica. His crooked teeth make her want to shrink inside herself. "You ready to meet those assholes at the clinic? Well, you better be."

He turns away and Wanda shoves past him with a pair of shoes. "Put these on, Jessica, and hurry. We can't keep the therapy people waiting anymore."

Jessica takes the shoes and hesitates. She hates anything tight on her feet and she sees Wanda has the shoes laced already. Anxiety increases in Jessica, and she wants to scream but shakes her head instead, then pushes the shoes away.

"Oh no you don't!" Wanda says, pushing the shoes back toward her.

Jessica jumps from the bed and runs for the door but before she gets out, Carl is standing there. She looks up at him, his gnarled face with a scar down the cheek stares back at her. She sees his chest rise and his cigarette-tainted breath falls on her in quick succession.

"I don't know what's going on here, but it stops now!" He looks at Wanda, who is standing behind Jessica now.

Wanda grabs Jessica's arm hard and pushes her through the door past Carl and into the living room. "We'll be ready in a minute." The bird squawks loudly, sending chills through Jessica. "Shut the hell up, Claw. I don't need to hear from you today."

"Shut the hell up, shut the hell up," Claw repeats, jumping wildly from one side to the other on his perch.

"Be careful not to put bruises on her arm," Carl says. "We don't need anyone asking questions or poking around here."

Jessica hears his protests but can see immediately they fall on Wanda's deaf ears.

She drops Jessica hard onto the old couch in the living room and the scratchy fabric touches her skin. It's worse than the bed. The couch feels like little needles are going through her everywhere.

Wanda crouches in front of her and shoves the shoes onto her feet. The couch and the shoes produce a fresh wave of painful sensations through Jessica, making her scream inside. She instinctively swats at Wanda's head, but the woman ducks and knocks them away.

Tears roll down Jessica's cheeks. She wants to retreat into her mirror dream where the old house waits, and the children speak. Any place but here. Her body is on fire, and she can do nothing to stop it.

Wanda stands and, before Jessica can run, the woman is shoving Jessica's arms into a coat. "Here, get this on. It's cold as hell out there."

"It's cold as hell out there," Claw says frantically.

Jessica feels it couldn't be much worse than in the house. The heat rarely works, and her bedroom is like being in a refrigerator.

Much worse than the rest of the place.

She is suddenly whisked toward the door, pushed forward against her will. Jessica tries to smack Wanda, and this time connects with the back of her head. Wanda turns on her and raises a hand, but before she can strike, Carl steps between them, grabbing Wanda's arm.

"That's enough! I done told you woman, no bruises. Get me?"

Wanda is seething, breathing hard, as she looks at Carl and then Jessica. She pulls her arm away. "Whatever. She's ready then."

Carl smiles, looking down at Jessica who feels less inclined to fight now. She turns for the door instead. Carl opens it and Wanda pushes Jessica out. The cold is shocking to Jessica's system. The temperature has dropped even more than yesterday, and small flakes of snow are blowing in the air.

Her breath is taken as she walks onto the porch.

The drab gray sky suits her mood as she walks toward the car. Jessica gets in the back and Wanda closes the door. Carl is sitting behind the wheel and glances through the rear-view mirror at her. Jessica sees the cold stare. He says nothing, only continues to look ahead.

For a moment, she thinks she sees yellow eyes in the mirror, but they vanish quickly.

A chill invades her body, and she feels like she is not alone in the backseat. This fades as her stomach reminds her that she hasn't had breakfast yet—a fact Wanda and Carl both seem to have forgotten—and her world is suddenly even gloomier than the outside scene.

She stares at the rows of dilapidated houses lining the street. A couple are boarded up and will probably be torn down like several of the others in this neighborhood. The result of what Carl likes to say is cooking. This brings thoughts of food to her mind again and she wishes she could push it away.

The car door opens on the passenger side and a fresh gust of cold winter air blows into the backseat where Jessica sits. She hugs herself and shivers run through her body. As the car moves forward, no one says a word.

For Jessica, this is the routine. Three days a week in therapy, with Carl and Wanda forgetting to take her until the clinic calls and they are afraid of being turned in to Social Services.

She would be just as happy if they didn't take her, and she could hide in her room.

Maybe dream and go back to where this world goes away.

Three
Renay

A pole with a large sign on top displaying "Carskills Rehab Center" lies ahead like a lighthouse beacon offering some form of refuge from the cold of the car. The heater barely works and it's even worse in the backseat. In there, the noises and lights are intense, but at least she'll be warm. The car pulls up to a stop near the front in the handicapped section where Carl always parks, taking advantage of the sign with the wheelchair man hanging from the front mirror.

The ride over had interested Jessica. Carl spoke like she wasn't there—always thinking she couldn't hear—and told a story about someone Jessica didn't know. The details were muddled and Jessica tuned it out while listening to the man on the radio talk about the approaching bad weather

Wanda gets out first and goes to the back door then opens it for Jessica. "C'mon, sweetie, it's time for your appointment," she says, and Jessica can hear the sudden change in her voice. The same as always when Wanda thinks someone is around. Jessica shivers so much her teeth chatter as she steps from the car. Carl is already at the facility's door. He opens it and goes in, leaving Wanda and Jessica outside like they aren't even there. Wanda grabs Jessica by the hand and shuffles forward like she's taking a kid to their first day of school.

Jessica pulls her hood over her head before they go in and Wanda protests. "I just combed your hair before we left the house and now you're going to cover it up?" She says but stops talking. Jessica knows it's because Wanda is afraid people will say something and make her look bad.

They step through the door and are greeted with a blast of thankful heat. The waiting room is bright and cheery with a Christmas tree flashing in the corner. Sponge Bob Square Pants is playing on the television hanging on the wall. Jessica suddenly finds herself mesmerized by this.

Carl sits below the monitor with his phone in his hand, paying no attention to anyone or anything. Jessica tries to break away from Wanda but feels her grip get tighter. Wanda produces a toothy smile and Jessica notices a few of her teeth are black. The woman has never had great teeth, but her appearance seems to be deteriorating lately, along with her weight. The tremors are more noticeable too, especially when she's nervous like she is now.

"Hi, we're here for her regular appointment," she says. Jessica hears the change in her voice. The same she used outside. This is when Wanda thinks she shines but Jessica, like everyone else, knows it's fake.

"Okay, I'll let Jonathan know," the lady behind the reception desk says. Jessica knows from past meetings the receptionist is Ruby. She's a portly woman with rosy cheeks and big hair. Jessica likes her because she always gives her a piece of candy when they are done. A low growl emanates from Jessica's stomach, and she wishes she could get the treat earlier today. Ruby leaves the desk and goes through a door to the gym room.

Jessica hasn't been here in a couple of weeks, but she remembers the inside of the center well. The lights are too bright, and she likes to put her hood over her head to make it dimmer. The people are nice, especially her therapist, Jonathan. He likes to tell jokes and make fun of the other girls in the gym, Trish and Brenda. They laugh back at him before going on about their business.

Sometimes Jessica would work with Brenda but not Trish. Something about her not specializing in the right therapy. Jessica had no idea what that meant.

Jessica stands there, rocking, engrossed in the television. She doesn't notice the door to the gym open but hears Jonathan's voice suddenly and turns. Jessica stares curiously, not at him, but at the girl beside him.

She's never seen her before, and it makes her nervous. The girl seems to be feeling the same thing as she studies Jessica for a moment. Something about her doesn't seem right to Jessica, like she's sad inside for some reason. Jessica is good at reading people and this girl is an open book. Her emotions are off the charts and Jessica is instantly on guard.

"Hey, Jess," Jonathan says, kneeling in front of her. "This is Renay. She's our new Occupational Therapist and she'll be working with you today."

Jessica stares flatly at her, showing no emotion only curiosity, like a cat sizing up prey. New things have a way of doing this to Jessica and she's not sure if she wants to work with this girl. Renay is slim, taller than the other girls, and has a warm smile but Jessica can tell it's fake. A cover-up for how she really feels. Her brown hair flows over her shoulders as she kneels beside Jonathan to talk to Jessica.

"Hi, I've heard good things about you from Jonathan. I think we'll be awesome friends," she says. Her eyes are bright.

Facial expressions are as important as words to Jessica, and she has a good, but reserved feeling towards Renay. Jessica does find it strange though, Jonathan said good things about her. The last time they were together, Jessica threw a fit when confronted by the mirror in the therapy gym.

This was shortly after her first trip inside, and she wanted to go back. The mirror was a distraction from her therapy, and she felt as though Jonathan was taking her away from what she wanted. Jonathan finally relented and Jessica was happy until she saw the yellow eyes staring back at her. It scared her and she screamed which resulted in her being taken away.

Jessica reaches for Jonathan's hand. She takes it, turning from Renay like she's not there. Her shield is up and will stay high until she gets a better read on this stranger.

Jessica watches as Jonathan shrugs to Renay and she produces a half smile, nodding to him.

Jonathan opens the door to the gym and Jessica feels the familiar tug of a hand prodding her forward. Jonathan's is much lighter than Wanda's though. He's also not nervous. The sensations Wanda gives off are enough to send Jessica to the ceiling.

Jonathan makes her feel calmer and less on edge. It's a good feeling and one she relishes.

The gym is full of color and the lights are so bright it makes Jessica wince. She releases her hand from Jonathan's and uses both to pull her hoodie tighter. The treatment room they usually go to is across the room. There is only one light in there and even though it's bright, the effect is a little more palpable and easier to handle for Jessica. Jonathan also plays music on his laptop. It's a soothing kind with no words.

It reminds Jessica of a bookstore she went to when with another foster parent. It was in another town with a big name she couldn't remember. The thought of a water tower always came to her when she thought about that time in her life. One with a big "C" at the beginning. The sign outside the bookstore said Wheatberry and Jessica thought it strange that wheat had berries.

Inside it smelled strange, like a mix of flowers and mailed letters, which soothed Jessica and made her feel warm and invited.

Oddly, the books with all of their vibrant colors didn't bother her the way they usually did. Music played overhead and calmed her senses, lulling her into relaxation. It was a memory she liked to go to now and then when things got too stressful.

Jonathan leads her into the treatment room, and she sits on the floor while he adjusts the laptop. Renay smiles at her and Jessica returns it with her usual cold stare.

A sheet covers the mirror behind the door and Jessica sees they aren't taking chances this time. Shivers of cold run up her back and she looks away from the place. Jonathan sits beside her with Renay on the other side, observing. "Hey, Jessica. Let's start by doing some brushing first."

Jessica smiles at this. The brush against her skin makes her happy, soothing her, unlike the brush Wanda runs through her hair when they are late. Jonathan places it firmly against her skin and the bristles lay flat, as he moves it down in a rhythmic fashion, causing her to relax and open her mind. A thump suddenly invades her ears like a bird hitting a window. She doesn't jump though, neither does she flinch. Jonathan and Renay don't seem to notice.

Where is it coming from? Her thoughts wander all over the place, and the brush—although making her feel better—seems to be opening her senses to other strange things. She pinpoints the sound. It's coming from the mirror behind the sheet. A strange aura begins to encapsulate Renay and Jessica stares at her strangely.

Light, streaming in different colors, flows from the sides of the covering and Jessica hears a whisper. The same as the children she's heard before.

Take the sheet away and we can play. Jessica, we want to talk to you, please. Take it down so we can see you.

Jessica reaches forward, away from Jonathan. The motion is slow like swimming through glue, and she is suddenly in another world. Jonathon tugs on her, trying to keep her still but she won't be denied her prize.

Jessica grabs the sheet and pulls it down.

Voices fill her head, as children laugh hysterically. They speak but it's unintelligible and comes in incoherent cackles. One voice stands out though above the others much deeper and older. Jessica hears it clearly but it speaks in an odd way.

"Open, inside you see, seek, find."

Four
Inside the Looking Glass

Colors flood Jessica's vision, and butterflies flutter in her stomach as the mirror draws her in. She's shocked to see Renay is going with her, though. Slowly, they get dragged forward, and Jessica watches as Renay stretches, elongating like a fun mirror until her shape is gone. The vibrant array intensifies until all she sees is one bright white light, making it impossible to see anything else, before all goes dark.

Jessica squints, trying to adjust her vision and sees Renay's bewildered stare looking back at her. Meanwhile, a half-light is coming from a rectangular portal to her side, appearing to be similar to a strange movie screen with amorphous shadows darting back and forth.

Renay reaches for it, touching the thing, but it doesn't give. Renay's fingers patter, sounding much like rapping against a car window.

She turns to Jessica, her eyes wide and panicky, "Where are we? What is this place?"

Jessica opens her mouth, but instead of grunts, her voice comes out as clear as the sky on a September day. Just like the last time she was here. "It's inside the mirror. The upside-down place. I come here sometimes to get away. No one's ever come with me, though."

"What do you mean? Inside the mirror. How's that possible? Wait, you can talk?"

The confused scrunch of Renay's face is funny and Jessica giggles when she talks to her. "Yes, inside the mirror, and yes, I can talk. Well, only in here I suppose." Jessica whips her head from side to side, excitably, then concentrates on the dark. "C'mon, let's go." She stands and takes a sure step to the nothing behind them.

"Wait," Renay calls out, but Jessica ignores her and continues forward. The voices of the children call to her, prodding her in the direction she should go. Jessica knows where they are taking her, even if Renay does not.

The house floats in its nest ahead and she's going to it with or without Renay.

A strange warmth takes over Jessica's body each time she sees it like the mirror house is a place of comfort, unlike her real home.

While inside the mirror, Jessica is boosted to another level. One of strength and endless possibilities without the hindrance of the real world. She's ignited and her excitement spurs her to explore this world that shouldn't be.

Dim light permeates the darkness, and Jessica stops in her tracks, then turns to Renay to point in the direction of the pinprick of light shining through the unimaginable darkness.

"It's right over there."

Renay shakes her head, clearly unable to understand. "What's there? I don't see anything."

"You will soon, C'mon!"

Jessica runs headlong into the dimness and comes to a grove of shrubs. A path stretches between them, and she can see the outline of the house silhouetted on the horizon. Jessica ducks under the bushes and takes the path, with Renay following, trying to keep up the best she can.

"Ahhh," Renay cries out.

Jessica turns to see that her companion had fallen to her knees. When she realizes nothing truly bad has happened, she speeds up again while Renay finds her footing and stumbles forward.

"Jessica! Slow down. Where are we going?"

Jessica laughs, too giddy with the desire to find the house again, ignoring Renay's question. She runs to the end of the shrubbery and sees a field ahead. The grass stretches over a sea of night with the tips of the blades glowing from some unseen light source.

They are like little fingers massaging the night sky, searching for a substance that isn't there. The ground below them is as blank as the sky above like they grow from black paint spilled onto a never-ending canvas ready to create some unknown art.

Only then does she notice the house positioned in a way that shouldn't be possible. Jessica gawks at the apparition ahead of her.

Renay steps up beside her, staring unbelievingly toward the house.

"What is it?"

Jessica purses her lips and gives Renay a sideways glance. "It's an upside-down house. What do you think it is?"

Renay starts to say something, but Jessica doesn't give her time to form the words before she's on her way through the field with an assurance only an innocent child can muster. She leaps over the tall bunches of grass like a deer running from hunters. Once she reaches the front yard of the place, she stops.

Renay catches up seconds later, panting, staring up at the structure with wide eyes.

"What's in there?" Renay asks.

Jessica turns to her and shakes her head. "I don't know, I've only been in the front yard.

"This is all so crazy. Where the hell are we?" Renay says, sounding like she's talking more to herself than Jessica.

"It's the mirror, silly. We're inside the mirror," Jessica says.

"I get that, but how is it possible?" Renay asks.

Jessica shrugs. "It just is."

Renay moves past her, heading toward the house. The voices become louder.

"What is that? Those noises. They sound like kids."

"They are. Those are my friends I talk to when I'm here. They tell me to go in the house, but every time I try, I wake up," Jessica says.

"So, this is like a dream?" Renay asks.

"I don't know. I guess so," Jessica replies. "Maybe like a dream where you know what you're doing."

"Like a lucid dream," Renay says.

Jessica shrugs. "I guess, even though I don't know what you're talking about."

Renay chuckles lightly and steps closer to the structure, studying the house and its strange upside-down appearance. Jessica watches her as Renay stretches her neck to see how far the stone foundation goes around the perimeter of the house, then she looks at the place itself.

"Why are the windows covered with mirrors?" Renay asks.

"I don't know. Why is the house upside down?" Jessica says.

"Good point, but it's all very strange and I'm wondering when we'll wake up. Are you controlling that aspect of things? Like can you pinch yourself and wake us up?" Renay asks, turning to Jessica.

Jessica laughs. "I don't think so, but why would I want to?"

Renay seems taken aback by the statement but asks no more, only stares in awe at the house's strange position. The children's voices go up in volume, attracting Jessica and Renay's attention to the small stones. They talk in unison, in a singsong fashion.

Come inside, we can play, come inside, and with us stay.

Jessica leaps past Renay but barely gets to the house when Renay is on her heels. They both step over the foundation at the same time, landing on what seems like nothing, but it solidifies under their feet.

Suddenly, they are standing on the steps of a right side up house.

Jessica scans the house, while Renay pants next to her. Her eyes are wide like some bewildered animal.

"What the hell just happened?" Renay asks.

"I don't know. I guess we're in front of the house. I've never been here before."

Jessica shivers like she's standing outside without a coat on, then she walks up the remaining steps and stops on the front porch. The boards ripple with energy below her feet with lights pouring up from the cracks beneath, blinking in and out like sparks in a fire, crackling with the intent to get larger. Renay reaches her side, staring at her feet in complete amazement or fear, Jessica can't tell.

Jessica steps closer to the outside wall of the house and looks inside one of the mirrors. At first, she sees her reflection as expected, but then it changes to a room with children playing. They dance in a circle with disjointed movements like weird ballerinas, singing a haunted melody although their mouths are closed.

Some have their hands in the air and others hold their arms tight against their sides, forming together like a flock of geese in a V-shaped pattern.

Before long, they stop and turn in unison to look at Jessica. Large, black eyes peer at her, a strange contrast against their pallid skin. Each has a black mark on their face like it was painted there.

Jessica looks away for a moment and sees Renay looking in a mirror as well. Instead of smiling, though, Renay frowns. She shrugs and turns to her own mirror window and notices the kids are retreating to their circle in the middle of the room. Jessica taps on the glass trying to get their attention again, but they ignore her as if she is not there.

"Come back," Jessica says, but they pay no attention.

Renay screams.

FIVE
RENAY'S MEMORIES

Renay's reflection stares back at her before the image fades into a strange world of half-truths. But it's her reality; the one she's tried to forget. Blood drips from the walls, dark red, leaving a stain of black emotion. The image changes to reveal the old house she once lived in. She remembers this day and, thankfully, recalls the fact that Trevor, her only son, is currently at his grandma's house.

In this memory reflected back to her, she is all alone. Pregnant, yes, but alone otherwise.

She sees herself walking cautiously around a corner, holding her very pregnant belly. Then there it is, the thing she doesn't want to see. Her ex-husband lying broken across his old recliner. The game playing on the large television overhead. Blood drips from the fingertips of Mike's extended arm hanging over the chair, and onto the floor beside him. It pools there and runs in all directions like a meandering river. Renay is taken aback by the amount of blood, and she feels a kick in her middle.

The baby is moving in response to her heartbeat, and she can't contain the feelings welling inside of her. She falls to her knees while watching Mike's boyfriend, Steve, point the gun in her direction. His eyes are destitute with no emotion. He lowers it for a moment, then brings it to his mouth.

Renay is frozen, unable to focus on the gruesome scene in front of her because her body is sending sharp, jabbing pains through her. She grabs her stomach and grimaces, squeezing, trying to muster up the energy to make it stop. The pain is so intense. She shakes her head slowly as the gun enters Steve's mouth, unable to look away at the horror she knows she's about to witness. Her cries for the vision to abate, along with the pain in her abdomen, go on deaf ears.

Steve pulls the trigger, and the back of his head explodes onto the screen behind him.

The announcer exclaims jubilantly the touchdown Ohio State completes, while bits of Steve run slowly down the screen, but Renay can barely hear any of it. Her ears are consumed with the sound of frantic beating in her chest and the all-encompassing pain in her midsection.

"Molly, please, baby. Stop," she pleads, but the sharp stabbing only continues until she's crumpled on the floor. She feels something wet between her legs and the movements inside her slow. Blood is all over the floor, coming closer to her, threatening to take over her world. She reaches to her middle and pulls back bloody fingers.

Shadows roll into her vision and a sudden pressure builds in her abdomen like she's going through the birth process. Renay screams when she sees a black arm, larger than a baby emerge from her. It grasps at the floor, trying to get out, then turns and grabs her. She cries out before falling backward.

Distorted visions cloud her thoughts, and all becomes bright again. She feels arms on her and frantic voices fill her ears.

The most prominent is Jonathan's.

"Renay? Are you okay? What happened?"

Renay rises to a sitting position and looks around. She's shaking so much her teeth chatter. Jessica is close by, crying and moaning, trying to say something but the words won't come out. A stark contrast from what Renay saw only moments ago. Trish is trying to console her, but Jessica is fighting to get away.

"What the hell is going on?" Jessica's dad bellows as he rushes into the treatment room.

"Carl. Stop. We have this under control," Jonathan says to him.

"I doubt that. This looks like anything but having it under control. Why is she crying?" he asks, then looks at the sheet beside the mirror on the door. "You know that upsets her. Why did you take it down?"

Jonathan sighs, then breathes in, "I didn't. It ... fell on its own."

"Then you should've secured it better. This is on you. You run this shit show. I'm taking her home and we ain't ever coming back. You'll hear from someone about this."

Wanda takes Jessica from Trish and helps her to stand.

Carl pats Jessica on the shoulder. "C'mon girl, let's get you out of this crazy-ass place."

Renay watches them leave, still in awe of what she experienced along with this girl.

Her nerves are on edge and her breath is coming quickly as she tries to calm down.

Trish puts a hand on her. "Oh my, you're shaking. What happened? I mean you were out for a good five minutes. We called 911. An ambulance is on its way."

Renay shakes her head. "I don't need it. I'm fine. It's just what I saw shook me up a bit."

"Well, that's what we need to talk about," Jonathan says. "Trish? Can you let Ruby know we're about to have a meeting and to hold treatments for a bit. I'll let her know when we're ready."

Trish stands. "Sure. Be back in a second."

Before she can leave, two paramedics enter the treatment room with a cot and oxygen canister.

Jonathan stands to greet them. "Hey, I'm Jonathan Burton, the owner of the clinic. Glad you got here so soon."

The paramedic nods and looks past Jonathan. "Is this the patient?"

"Yes, but I think she's going to be fine. She's shaken up a bit but seems to be good now. I'm canceling her patients for the day and letting her rest."

"No, that won't be necessary," Renay says. "Give me a minute and I'll be good."

"Can we at least give an assessment?" the paramedic asks.

"Okay, but I don't need it." Renay protests.

The paramedic checks her vitals and enters the findings into his tablet before he turns to Renay. "Everything looks good, but it looks like all of the blood has been drained from you. You definitely need rest."

"Thank you," Jonathan says.

The paramedics pack up their gear and head out the door. Soon Renay is sitting in the office at her desk, drinking from a bottle of water Ruby brought. Trish, Brenda, and Jonathan sit across from her, waiting for her to finish.

"Okay, now what exactly happened to cause you and Jessica to black out? I know the mirror distresses her, but this time it affected you as well," Jonathan says.

Renay sighs. "I don't know. One minute I was here and the next I was dreaming."

"Dreaming?" Trish asks.

"Yes. That's the only way I can explain it," Renay says, leaving out the part about the house and the strange world behind the mirror. She supposes it was all a dream, but until she can decipher what really happened, she'll concentrate on what caused the outburst. "I know I've only been here a short time, and you all know I'm a widow and about my boy Trevor, but there's more to the story," Renay says. "My husband ... well, my ex-husband ... died. He had a lover I didn't know about, and it rocked my world. He took care of me and Trevor though, never letting us go without. He was a responsible man in that way at least," she says, looking at the floor. "I don't know how to say this. There must have been more going on than I knew about because Mike was killed by his lover, Steve, in a murder-suicide situation."

Jonathan's eyes widen, then he reaches over to pat Renay on the hand. "Oh man, I'm so sorry," he says.

Renay nods. "Thank you, but there's more to the story. You see, I witnessed the whole thing while pregnant with a little girl."

"That's horrible," Trish says.

"Yeah, it was. I had such plans for Molly. My Molly Renay, I called her while I patted my belly. I sang songs to her every day and Trevor was so excited to be a big brother. But that day changed everything. When Mike and Steve died, it was the end of Mike's support and the death of my baby."

"Oh God," Trish says. "You lost the baby?"

Renay sniffs, recalling the pain once again; the thoughts still hanging in her recent memory. "I did. Molly would be nearly two years old today and I would more than likely be at home holding her." Renay shrugs. "I suddenly had more responsibility laid upon me and a baby to bury. You see, she was nearly full term."

"I can't imagine how horrible that would be," Brenda says.

Tears well in Renay's eyes as she recalls the day, she laid her baby to rest. The cold solemn process with only her, Trevor, and her mom. Winter had come and it was close to Christmas. The following months would be much colder than the wind blowing across the cemetery. Therapy sessions and days away from Trevor became the norm for a while. She got through it, though, and even managed to forget some of it, until now.

Christmas was nearly here again, and the pain had come front and center. Even the anti-depressants prescribed to aid in those problems, wouldn't fix this.

"Well, I'm glad you let us know," Jonathan says. "I'm letting you go home for the day. You need rest, and don't try and talk me out of it. It's Thursday and I know you go home on Fridays anyway. So, get an early start and go see your boy and your mom. Come back Monday, fresh and ready to start."

"I don't think that's necessary but—"

"Like I said, don't try and talk me out of it. I won't change my mind," Jonathan interrupts her.

"He's right, sweetie," Trish says. "You should get some rest."

Renay nods, hesitantly. "Okay. I'll gather my things. Thank you so much for understanding."

In a few minutes, Renay heads out the door.

Six
The Looking

The ride home from the clinic makes Jessica cry. She doesn't know why everyone is so upset. Sure, she made a scene, but so did Renay. In Jessica's eyes, no one is at fault, except for the quick, angered reactions of Carl and Wanda.

The house is as cold as the outside when they arrive and Jessica wonders if they forgot to pay the electric bill again. The pair have a way of forgetting so many things. Sometimes she doesn't understand why they have her in the first place and if she would be better served by another set of parents.

Wanda has told her countless times that her real mother is plastered on a missing persons poster, but Jessica has never seen it.

Jessica goes straight to her room and grabs a blanket off the bed, then wraps it around her. She lowers herself in front of the mirror, while her foster parents are talking outside in the next room. Jessica can't help but overhear what they are saying through the thin walls.

"Who are you talking to," Wanda says.

"None of your fucking business," Carl spits back to her.

It's always the same interaction. Wanda questions and Carl beats her down with words and sometimes fists.

She hears Carl's footsteps coming closer, heading toward the bathroom at the end of the hall next to her room, while he's talking to someone.

"Yeah, let's get this done as soon as possible," he says, then hesitates. "That's right, same cut as before." There's a pause, then Jessica hears the door to the bathroom shut and the conversation becomes muffled.

Jessica wonders who he's talking to but figures it's something she doesn't want to know about. Wanda and Carl do a lot of things like that, so she stays out of their way as much as possible. After today, though, her mind is on fire, and she wants nothing more than to go back to the mirror where she can yell across the vast darkness and maybe go into the house.

A gust of heat hits her legs and she's relieved to see it still works. She pulls the blanket tight around her shoulders and soaks up as much of the warmth as she can.

The mirror shows nothing more than her reflection, so she concentrates on the edge where the bend of light is located. Her mind wanders there, and she lets go. The tension from earlier dissipates, slowly relaxing her muscles, the worries flowing out of her.

Soon, colors flood her mind—red, orange, yellow, green, and blue—stretching away and combining to become one brilliant rope of mashed light. Jessica feels the very familiar tug on her body and her consciousness fades while she allows it to take her into the mirror world.

Jessica breathes in and out slowly, like *meditating*—the word her therapists call it.

They tell her to relax when she is stressed.

This doesn't always work but in the upside-down place, all things are possible.

She closes her eyes for a second and when she opens them again, she's there.

The dark behind her and the dim light of the glass portal in front.

On the other side of the mirror, she sees her physical form crouching. She's always concerned someone could harm or take her body while her mind is in this state, this wonderful and surreal place. Then again, Carl and Wanda are so wrapped up in their petty lives that she doubts they'll even notice. If they did, they would probably look at it as a way to enjoy some peace from the troubled girl in their house.

Jessica stands and turns her attention to the place where the children call to her. She can't wait to get back to the house, and maybe this time, she can go in. Without further thought, she disappears into the darkness.

"It's all set," Carl says jubilantly, as he walks into the kitchen.

Wanda sits at the table, fiddling nervously with a needle. She jumps and nearly knicks her bicep instead of the plump vein produced by the tied cloth on her arm.

"Dammit, Carl? You scared the shit out of me."

Carl shakes his head. "I can't believe you mess with that shit. Why don't you take a pill like everyone else," he says. Carl yanks open the fridge door and pulls out a can of beer. He cracks the lid open and takes a swig, then belches. Carl leans against the countertop and smiles. "All our troubles will be a distant memory once we get rid of her."

Wanda looks at him strangely while inserting the needle into the crease of her elbow. She shivers when she pushes the plunger down. "Carl, you know we can't do that. You remember what that thing said to you," she says. Her head ticks slightly and her eyes widen. "It scares me when you talk about it."

"Listen, I got this. We're going to do a trade. One child for another. Bresnik says that should please it enough to get our boy back."

Wanda stares at the needle she's placed beside her on the table. Her eyes are sad. "Bresnik? What's that bastard know? He's the reason we're in this shape to begin with.

I thought the girl would help but it doesn't. I want my Timmy back. We wouldn't have her if my sister was smart enough not to get in with those rich men.

She's nothing but a fading poster on a light pole now and I have to raise her daughter."

Carl turns and steps toward the window.

He takes another drink from his beer and then sighs. "I know it's not easy, but we'll get Timmy. I'm sure of it."

"How you gonna do that, Carl? Bresnik took us there in the first place and he's the reason we lost Timmy. All that shit about he didn't know what would happen. He knew. That man always has something up his sleeve."

"You think I don't know that? The whole situation is as screwed up as any I ever heard. If you hadn't needed to go to Kentucky and try to get your sister back, we could've avoided the whole thing.

Damn, Wanda, why couldn't you let it go? She was long dead before we even got there."

"Because, she was my sister, you bastard. I loved her and wanted her back, not her kid and I sure didn't want to lose mine."

"Whatever, that's old news, but don't worry, I'm going to fix it. Now, shut up and go to sleep. That shit'll be hitting you soon."

Carl grabs another beer before he storms away.

Wanda thinks about her boy and wonders if Carl has any clue about what he's doing.

The thought clings to her for a moment, then she shakes it off and instead makes her way to the couch in the living room. Wanda falls onto it and lets the world fade away.

Seven
I See You

Jessica runs through the dark meadow toward the house. When she gets there, she stands in front of the stones. She hadn't noticed before but there were words written on each of them. Some are names she's never heard of, old names, like Helga and Ezekiel, but they were in the back. The newer ones in front had names like Peggy and the one closest to the front says, Timothy. Another had a bunch of writing Jessica didn't understand, like it was written in a foreign language.

She jumps onto the porch without a care and the house immediately rights itself like last time. Jessica runs up to the front door and grabs the handle of the door. It's a large ornate thing with a lion in the middle; the mane flowing all around it and curving to the back of the knob.

The door handle is the only thing on the house's exterior that can be considered fancy, aside from the mirrors adorning the outside, which have some interesting frames. The rest, however, is for the most part, plain.

She turns the handle and is surprised to find the door unlocked. She pushes it inward and listens for a second as the door creaks on old, worn hinges. Jessica steps inside and looks around. A dusty room greets her, and she jumps a little when she sees black bugs scurrying into corners from the sudden onslaught of light. Their path has no reason, and they disappear haphazardly into the walls.

Jessica walks slowly through the house and turns a corner. She sees a long hallway going straight and ending at some stairs.

Peeking cautiously into the hallway, she sees doorways on either side. One has a door and the other doesn't. She walks until she gets to the open one and she peeks inside.

The room is empty except for a dusty and worn table with cobwebs strewn across the top.

Satisfied, Jessica turns to the room with the door.

She opens it and her eyes widen. Inside, children sit in two rows in front of a large mirror, waiting patiently for something—perhaps a movie —to start. She steps inside and all heads turn at once, staring at her.

Then, from the corner of her vision, she sees a large figure stepping out of the shadows.

Jessica shudders at its appearance. It looks like a cricket on its lower half with legs set backward away from its body. It has black shoes on but the way they're turned makes them funny and out of place. The top half is an older woman with gray hair and black teeth jutting from her flat lipless mouth.

Her eyes are like the children's, dark and large, marble-like, ready to fall out and roll across the room if she moves too fast.

She's like a hag from a fairy tale, too odd to be believed. Jessica steps back as the witchy-looking creature skitters toward her like an insect. Small audible clicks strike the floor with each movement, sending cold chills over Jessica's body. It reminds her of the little bugs that run across her bedroom at night when the lights are out.

The woman stops in front of Jessica and raises a hand. She winces but the old woman doesn't attack her. She only motions for Jessica to sit with the rest of the children. She does so reluctantly, not taking her eyes off the old woman. The kids move to the side to let her in, and she sits cross-legged with them which is very strange with the way her legs are shaped. They fold in on themselves like she's curling up in a half-ball shape.

The mirror flashes a few beams of light but quickly starts to focus. Jessica squints and adjusts her eyes, then sees a figure in the glass, one of a woman she knows. It's Renay and she's lying on a bed with her back to the mirror and only a towel around her.

Jessica continues to watch and notices something else there. A shadow-looking thing appears, rolling ever closer to Renay.

It's like a fog falling over her and Jessica notices its yellow eyes, the same as she saw in her other encounters in the mirror. They are mesmerizing and capture her gaze momentarily. She sees slits like a cat in them and they blink strangely since there are no eyelids.

Jessica is so engrossed by the scene she fails to notice that around her the children are gone. She's all alone in the room watching Renay and, as the shadow falls across her, Jessica can feel small tendrils touch her skin in the same place they come in contact with Renay. The sensation is weird but not overwhelming like most touch is to her. In here, in the upside-down place, it doesn't seem to work that way.

Suddenly, Renay turns to see the shadow thing. She screams and throws the towel at the mirror. Jessica watches as it hits the glass and falls away. The next thing she sees is the back of Renay's naked body as she runs from the room.

Jessica shakes her head, unsure of what is happening but notices the thing in the mirror hasn't left. It's still there, floating in the room. It turns those yellow eyes to gaze at her, blazing against the backdrop of the black smokescreen. They consider her and blink a few times before fading away along with the shadow itself.

The mirror image of Renay's room fades as well, and Jessica is left looking at her own reflection. But there's another there, too. A little boy with sadness draped across his face is standing behind her, quietly looking over her shoulder.

His dark eyes bore into her like they wanted to consume her whole being. He opens his mouth, revealing a row of sharp teeth. He steps toward her, and she turns to look at him but he's not there. Jessica checks the mirror again but only sees her reflection.

She stands and stretches, then scans the room. The children are gone and she's all alone again.

The door she came through is shut so she goes to it. Jessica wants to explore the rest of the house and see what other treasures she can find. The place is dark, and she hears the scuttle of things in the walls. Other than that, a strange silence pervades the air around her.

She suddenly feels very lonely and longs to see the children again. Jessica turns the knob to the door and hears a clack indicating it's open. She pulls it to her and steps through quickly but instead of finding herself in the hallway, she's outside again.

Jessica looks up at the house back in its upside-down appearance. It hovers in silence, seeming shut to any more mysteries.

The stones on the ground beside it are silent too.

With a hefty sigh, Jessica figures it's time to go back to the real world. Not wanting to overstay her welcome, she walks back across the field of dark grass until she's in total darkness again. She closes her eyes and then wakes in her physical body.

Her room is quiet and dark, indicating the late hour. There is a low noise coming from somewhere else, though. It takes her a moment to realize she's hearing the television. Apparently, Wanda and Carl are engrossed in their own little world and, like always, she's been forgotten.

In a different life, this may have bothered her, but here and now ... it's the way she likes it.

EIGHT

THE MIRRORS ARE WATCHING

Renay wakes on the couch downstairs. She sits at attention, grabbing the blanket and pulling it to her neck. The thought of the thing she saw in the mirror lingers in her mind and she can't shake the fear she feels.

Light streams in through the cracks between the Venetian blinds. Her nakedness exposes her even if she's the only one here. The lingering thought in her mind says differently.

She wraps the blanket around her body as close as she can and ascends the stairs. At the top, she sees her bedroom, the door ajar. The full-length mirror reflects her image back at her and she hurries over to cover it with the blanket from her body.

Renay stands there for a moment, shivering. Did she see what she thought she saw last night? The eyes and the clawed hands—the same apparition she saw in the dream when she blacked out at the clinic.

Was it a dream? Yes, it had to be.

She hugs herself and rubs her skin to try and stay warm but realizes a hot shower would probably make things better. Renay makes her way to the bathroom and is startled when she glances at another mirror.

The one above the sink that attaches to the door. Without hesitation, she opens it and lets it fall to the side where she can't see her reflection anymore. This whole situation is grinding her nerves and she's ready to go home, and to take advantage of the few days off afforded to her.

Renay turns the handle for the shower and lets the water run until steam rises and rolls across the ceiling. The room warms and Renay relaxes slightly. She steps in and lets the water fall across her shoulders where she's been holding a lot of tension. The episode yesterday didn't help her mental health at all.

When she's done, she towels off and starts to close the door to the cabinet but thinks better of it. Renay makes her way to the bedroom, where she pulls her hair into the towel and folds the edges around until it's tightly around her head. She then picks up the phone, which she'd left on her nightstand that afternoon. Her mom has already called, of course. She places the phone on the bed and shivers while walking to the chest of drawers. While there, she grabs some clothes, underwear, jeans, and a large sweatshirt hoodie. Renay quickly puts everything on and takes the towel from her head. After she brushes the tangled mess out, she pulls it into a damp ponytail.

Before long, she's in her car with the heater blasting and a book of Occupational Therapy techniques playing over the sound system. It's so cold outside that she barely had time to get to the vehicle without the winter wind taking a bite out of her.

I should have dried my hair, she thinks. *Hindsight and all that jazz.*

December seems like it's going to be brutal already and the last thing she needs is to get sick. Hopefully, her hair will be dry before she gets out of the car again. Before she gets too comfortable with the warming car and tense novel, she asks her phone to call her mom.

The name Maddy the Great comes across the screen and the phone rings.

Maddy answers after the first two. "Hi, honey, are you on your way?"

"Yeah, Mom. I should be there in a couple of hours, maybe more if I stop for coffee. I figure I will," Renay says, chuckling. "How's Trev doing?"

"He's fine," Maddy says, then Renay hears the pleading of her son in the background.

"He wants to talk to you. Here he is."

"Hi, Mommy. Love you," the little voice comes over the phone. A cherubic sound if ever there was one.

"I love you, too. How's Mommy's big man? You taking care of Grandma?"

"We've been playing and I drawed something for you. Are you coming soon?"

Renay smiles. Her son is quite an artist and enjoys his outlet whenever he gets the chance, which is typically all the time. "Oh, I can't wait to see it. Yes, I'll be home soon, sweetie."

"Yay!"

"We'll get pizza and do something together when I get there."

"Pwomise?"

"I promise. Now, give the phone back to Grandma, please. Mommy loves you."

"Okay, Mommy, love you," he says, followed by kissy sounds. The sounds warm Renay more than any heater could. More than the sun could.

"He's been drawing quite a bit. Some things I can't even figure out."

"What do you mean?" Renay asks.

"I'll let you look at them when you get here. Don't worry about it now. See you soon, Renay."

"Alright, Mom. Love you."

"Love you too," Maddy says before hanging up.

Renay relaxes a bit, the weight lifting off her shoulders as she becomes more invested in her audiobook. Her mind wanders toward her patients. It's been a while since she'd practiced, but things were coming back to her. She had a client the other day whom she rocked gently in her lap to induce calm. She also did some light compression on the joints, following a brushing session, to provide proprioceptive feedback. The Wilbarger Brushing method is used by many practitioners, Jonathan included, and the results are phenomenal. Renay used it quite a bit during her clinical residency at Ohio State University. Back when she wanted nothing more than to be a pediatric therapist.

Jessica, though, while she had only met her once, made a lasting impression.

Already, Renay was rethinking everything she thought she knew about the field. Renay can only imagine what the poor thing goes through with the family dynamic she's up against. It's something to ponder and she's sure she'll get the chance when she gets back, but for now, Trevor is waiting.

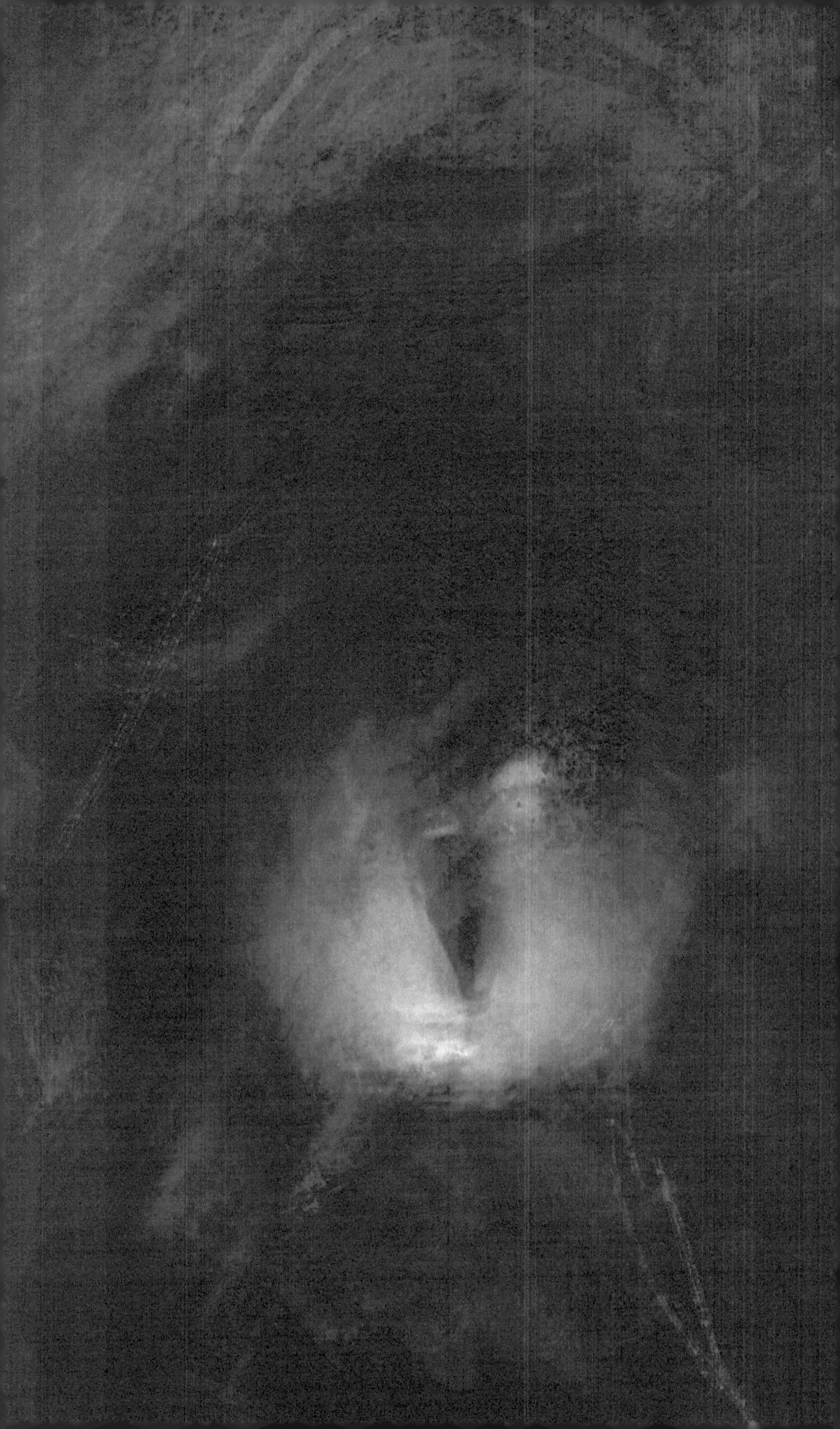

Nine
Jessica in the Basement

Jessica stares at the dull white ceiling, leaning toward yellow from the stains there.

It makes her sad in some way mostly because she's back here and not inside the mirror. She gets out of bed and stretches, then walks toward the kitchen. Claw makes noise in the shadow of the living room. She sees his silhouette and his craning neck.

"Hey, girl! Hey, girl!" The bird calls out to her.

"Shut up, you stupid bird," Carl yells.

Jessica ducks into the kitchen before Carl spots her and goes to the refrigerator, where she sees beer and a few bottled waters.

Jessica grabs one of the waters, then closes the door. As she turns, she sees Wanda sitting slumped at the kitchen table, clutching a picture in a frame. It's one Jessica has seen before. Wanda and Carl's son, who they lost a long time ago.

"You ask for that," she says. Her words slur slightly. "You know, he's got big plans for you. It won't be long now."

Jessica stares at Wanda unsure if she should go or stay. She decides to go and turns for her bedroom but stops when she sees Carl standing in the doorway.

He stares flatly at Jessica, then nods to Wanda. "Put her in the basement, I got someone coming over," he says.

Jessica shakes her head furiously. Not the basement. She hates it down there. The spiders hang in the corners and bugs crawl across the floor, and she can hear their legs scraping.

Jessica bolts for the hallway toward her room but can't make the distance before Wanda has a hand on her arm. She pulls away and Wanda falls against the wall with a thud.

Wanda curses but regains her resolve to capture Jessica and pins her sideways against the wall.

Claw moves back and forth in the next room, his wings flapping like he's ready to take off for the sky.

"Someone's coming, someone's coming," he screeches with a shrill voice.

Wanda huffs, breathing heavily like she's run a marathon from the small amount of exertion placed on her body.

"Listen, bitch, you're not pulling this shit on me," she says, taking a deep raspy breath, "Now, move your ass to the basement."

Wanda pushes Jessica along past her bedroom and down the hall to a door at the end. Jessica tries again to get away, but Wanda has her firmly by the arm and won't let go. Jessica is so mad, she bites her own arm hard.

"You can hurt yourself all you want. It won't do you any good," Wanda says.

With her free hand, Wanda opens the door and with the other, shoves Jessica onto the first step. Jessica reaches for the stair railing to maintain her balance. Tumbling down the stairs would be bad because she doubted they would help her if she got injured. Jessica is on her own here and she knows it.

The door slams shut behind her and she hears it lock. Wanda's raspy wheezing is loud on the other side as she walks away.

Jessica stands on the step for a moment, listening through the door the best she can.

Muffled voices can be heard and Claw shuffling around on his perch. He calls out his intruder alert warning and Jessica knows someone is out there.

She can do nothing about it. She screams at the top of her lungs but knows this is only in her mind as no sound is produced. Jessica hits herself hard on the side of her head multiple times. She then bites her arm again.

It's so frustrating that she can't get all the emotions out, like they're stuck in her head and won't release.

She finally stops and turns, extending her hand to fumble for the light switch on the wall, and finds it, flipping it up.

The steps below illuminate with a light-yellow hue. Jessica runs down the steps, nearly missing the last one. Cold invades her body along with the strange loneliness of a place she has no desire to go.

She has no shoes on, a fact Wanda or Carl care little about. They never seem to prioritize her health or theirs for that matter.

They live for each day like it's their last and Jessica figures, it may be.

She continues running until she gets to an old mattress in the middle of the room, then plops onto it. The whoosh of the cottony foam sends waves of unsettling sensations on her skin, causing her to smack herself again multiple times on the side of her head, then she bites her hand very hard, almost enough to bring blood, and begins to rock until she soothes herself.

Jessica releases the hand from between her teeth and gently sets it down in front of her.

She concentrates on it and twitches it quickly, nodding her head in quick succession until she finds the right pattern.

This relaxes her and she lets her thoughts wander.

Jessica has seen the picture Wanda was holding before. It's not something her foster mom talks about, but Jessica is aware that it brings Wanda great sadness.

Then, out of nowhere, she remembers the boy standing behind her when she was in the mirror. He'd had the same face as the one in the picture. The distortion of his eyes and mouth made him look a bit different, but it was him. Jessica *knows* it was him.

Footsteps go back and forth above, but the only sound she can make out is Claw's caterwauling.

It's not quiet enough to hear the bugs skittering around but she's sure those sounds will resume soon enough. Jessica stands and walks to a corner where a box of junk sits. Dust and cob-webs—probably with big spiders attached somewhere—cover the top and Jessica winces when she brushes them away. This is beyond her comfort zone, but the boredom is too much, and she has to do something.

Inside the old box are several items. Some children's books and a few baby toys. Maybe the ones belonging to the boy in Wanda's picture, she thinks. Jessica moves them to the side and sees some-thing strange at the bottom of the box.

It's shaped like a seashell. Something she's seen in books but never in real life. She pulls it out and blows on it. Fine particles fly through the air, settling on the box and the items inside.

The little thing has a clasp on the side, firmly fixing it shut. Taking it with both hands, Jessica pries it open. Inside is a small mirror. Glass lines the top and on the bottom is a beige-colored pad with a strange smell Jessica can't pinpoint, but it's similar to soap.

She doesn't care about it though, only the mirror. She looks at her reflection and wonders if she can get lost in there like she does with the big mirror.

Jessica takes it with her and goes back to the mattress. She sits and stares into the small mirror, concentrating as hard as she can. Small lights spark at the edge of the casing and Jessica smiles.

Suddenly, the confined space of the basement doesn't bother her as she relaxes and allows her mind to be immersed in the light and feels the familiar tug.

Ten
Homecoming

Renay gets into Columbus early in the afternoon. The sky is thick, pregnant gray clouds threatening to burst, and the smell of snow hangs heavily in the air. The wind picks up, and an angry gush of icy air makes her pull her hood around her head much tighter.

The more Northerly position of this city and the lack of hills make it much colder than Portsmouth. The noticeable difference is enough for Renay to wish she'd brought some of the warmer weather with her.

Christmas decorations adorn her mom's porch, a homey, jovial feeling resonating from the house. She smiles, the bad weather all but forgotten. She puts the car in park and reaches in the back seat for her bag of clean clothes. A basket of dirty clothes is in the trunk, but she'll get those later.

As Renay walks toward the house, she sees Trevor peeking from the blinds. He opens the door and comes bounding onto the porch before she can take the first step up the stairs. He nearly knocks her down when he grabs her around the middle for one of the best hugs she's ever gotten.

"Mommy! I missed you so much," he says, "I have pictures to show you. I've been drawing a bunch."

"I heard. I can't wait to see them."

Renay raises her head to see her mom standing at the open door. "He's been pacing by the window all day." She laughs. "How have you been, baby?"

A sigh escapes Renay's lips. "I'm tired Mom, but it's great to be home."

"I wish you could stay. Surely you can find work around here. Columbus has some of the best hospitals in the world."

"Mom, we've been through this," Renay says while walking past. "The jobs are here, but the pay isn't. I can make a bunch more as a traveler. I'll be off for three months, once the job is done. That is if I don't sign on for more."

Maddy closes the door once Trevor comes back inside. "Does that mean you'll be taking Trevor if that happens?" she asks.

"Mom, we've been through this part too," Renay huffs. "I'll only take him if I'm at the job for more than a year. I don't want him to be like some military brat. But at the same time, we need each other."

Maddy nods and walks toward the kitchen. "Coffee?" she asks.

"I would love some," Renay says.

"Okay, sit with Trevor and check out the pictures he's been dying to show you. I'll be in the kitchen."

Renay lays her bag on the chair in the corner. Her mom keeps this place spotless, and the bag looks out of place like it should be in a dorm room and not the pristine backdrop of Maddy's house. Renay remembers being scolded as a teenager for putting her book bag wherever it fell. Also, for having boys in her room and loud music playing or whatever her teenage rebellious years called for.

So many memories come back to her as she scans the room and sees pictures of her at every stage of growing up. The house is warm, inviting, and smells like home should.

Trevor is shuffling through a pile of papers at the table, so Renay makes her way there and sits beside him. He lines them up in some sort of order only he understands and motions for her to look.

"I drew this one today."

Renay looks at it and smiles. It's a picture of what she assumes is Maddy and Trevor decorating a Christmas tree. She knows her mom won't have one up for at least another week, but the anticipation on Trevor's face says, he's been asking.

"Oh, a Christmas tree. Are you excited for Christmas? You know Mommy has the whole week off? Maybe we can plan a vacation before I go back to work?"

Trevor's eyes light up at this announcement. "Can we go to the big pool with the slides? The wolf place?"

Renay realizes he's talking about Great Wolf Lodge in Cincinnati, and she may have been thinking the same. "That's fine with me. Grandma can go too. We'll swim until we become prunes."

Trevor laughs. "I'll swim and never get out of the water."

Renay smiles but then sees another picture peeking from under the first one. She pulls it out and studies it. A rectangle shape is in the middle of the paper and centered in the shape are squiggly lines. The form of someone is behind the lines with their hands reaching like they are trying to get through.

She inspects it closer and sees a girl in there with dark eyes. It's hard to tell exactly who the picture resembles. She squints, following the grouping of lines and squiggles. A hodgepodge of indiscriminate things going in different directions.

Without thinking, she pulls the next picture out and her heart sinks. An upside-down house, the same one from her shared dream with Jessica, is drawn in her son's crayons. She stares at it for a moment, levels her gaze at her son, and asks in a calm tone, "What's this supposed to be, honey?"

Trevor takes the paper from her and studies it then turns to Renay. "It's the house from my dreams."

Renay's heart begins beating faster. "Your dreams? When did you draw this?"

Trevor looks at her thoughtfully. "I don't know. Yesterday, I guess."

Chills run through Renay's body. The same day as her dream. This is too weird.

Not wanting to scare her son, she asks, "Can you remember the—"

Renay cuts herself off as Maddy comes in with two steaming mugs. She sits one beside Renay then walks to the other side of Trevor, pulling out a chair before sitting.

As if she notices the sudden shift in the room, Maddy looks at Renay. "What's wrong?"

Renay shakes her head. "The pictures, Mom," she says, then picks up the one with the house. "This one especially. Do you see the house in it? Notice anything odd about it?"

Maddy studies the paper. "It's an upside-down house. Why?"

"Mom, I dreamed of this place yesterday. Don't you think that's odd?"

"Not really. It only means you two are connected. You did give birth to him, and he was part of you for nine months. It only stands to reason you two would share a few things," Maddy says then takes a sip of her coffee, clearly unperturbed.

Her mother was probably right, of course.

As weird as the coincidence was, it could just be that—a coincidence.

She yawns and stretches. Looking at her phone, she sees it's already four PM. She shouldn't be tired but with all the events that have happened, Renay feels she needs a nap.

"Thanks for the coffee, Mom, but I think I'll take it with me upstairs. I need some rest."

Maddy nods. "Okay, sweetie. I'm sure it's been an eventful week. Get some rest and we'll talk in the morning or later this evening."

Renay pulls away from the table. Before she picks up her coffee, she leans in and hugs Trevor, then kisses his forehead. "Love you, little man. Mommy's going to take a nap, then we'll hang out and watch some TV."

"Okay, Mommy," Trevor says, then turns back to his picture. Renay grabs her coffee and disappears upstairs. Some rest will do her good. She has a lot to think about.

Eleven

A Different Path

The room is dark when Renay wakes. She's not ready to get up yet, so she grabs her phone, only to see that it's 2:00 AM. *Did she sleep for eight hours? It* doesn't seem possible but maybe the fatigue with all that had happened took its toll on her. She starts to pull up the Facebook app and is interrupted by a tapping sound. Renay instinctively looks to the window. There's a slight wind and things blowing around like a snowstorm may be brewing. The cold and quietness of the house is like a vacuum and Renay has no desire to get out from under the snug fit of her blanket and she pulls it closer as a shiver of fear goes through her body.

The tapping noise sounds again and the need to find it piques her interest but not her resolve to get out of bed. Yet she must find the source.

She eases from under the covers and places her feet on the rug, separating them from the cold hard surface of the hardwood floors. Renay slips her socks on and steps lightly toward the window, trying not to slip on the twice polished floors.

Renay's almost to the window when she hears the taping noise again but it's not coming from there this time, it's behind her.

Chills fill her body at the thought someone may be standing there. She eases around and sees nothing but her chest of drawers. The tapping becomes incessant, and Renay is taken with the instinct to run. Her legs are lead, though, so she concentrates on the source of the noise instead. It's coming from the mirror on top of the piece of furniture.

This isn't possible.

Renay takes a breath and walks closer to the mirror.

Light shadows arc inward around the edges of the frame, pulsating with energy, a wave going from black to gray and back again. She gasps when she hears a voice inside.

"Jessica? Is that you?"

The voice comes back in an echo and Renay turns her ear to listen.

"It's me. I need your help," she says.

Renay shudders at the sound of fear in Jessica's voice. Not only is she dealing with the impossibility of the world beyond but also the real possibility Jessica may be in danger.

"Jessica? Come to my voice," Renay calls out, then listens.

Silence answers her for a good long moment.

"I can't find my way. It's not like the last time. This is different with a mirror I'm not familiar with. Please help!" The fear is palpable in Jessica's voice.

She places her fingers on the glass and watches as they disappear. Her fingertips are cold from whatever strange energy is on the other side. Renay goes farther and feels her whole hand being pulled inside.

"Well, in for a penny, in for a pound," she says out loud. One of her mom's sayings.

Renay hoists herself up to sit on the top of the chest of drawers, hearing it creak slightly from her weight. She lets herself fall backward into the abyss, holding on with her hands to the dresser long enough until she thinks she can control her descent. Renay gets as far in as she can, then let's go, and feels herself tumble out of control into the mirror behind her.

Renay stops and notices the ground she cannot see below her is solid. She's sitting with her hands extended behind her keeping her upright. The strangeness of the lack of a clearly defined ceiling and floor is disorienting, but she concentrates on getting her bearings.

Renay stands and stretches, extending her hands in front of her, feeling nothing solid.

She steps uncertainly into the nothingness.

This is so different from the last time she was in the mirror world. Then, she saw light coming from the opening she'd gone through, but this time, the area was devoid of any. This only added to her tension.

Renay hears a light thrum in her ears like a slight ringing; one you barely hear but you still know it's there. Something electric fills the air and her hair rises slightly like the static from a sweater in the winter.

Fear rises in her and she's consumed with the thought she's being watched. Yellow eyes appear in front of her, cat-like, studying her like they are sizing her up for dinner.

Renay's heart thuds in her chest and she takes a step backward before she goes into a full run.

Jessica hears things this time in the mirror, but oddly, not the children. They've always guided her way before but not this time. A thrumming sound invades her ears, and her senses are on high alert. The darkness is all-consuming and makes it hard to find her way. She wants out now. This isn't like the last times, and it scares her, a sense she doesn't understand. The extra confusion makes this even more difficult.

She does the only thing she can think of and calls out to Renay, but Jessica hears nothing and continues to wander a little farther into the shadowy depths of nowhere.

She extends her hands in front of her, hoping to find something solid. There is nothing there and panic begins to build inside her. She wants to run and never stop but is afraid of what may be out there in the dark. She hears a swoosh sound close by and turns her head in that direction. Jessica reaches toward the area but it's not solid, so, she calls for Renay again and hears nothing.

If only she could find the house and the children's voices to guide her.

Jessica cries out to Renay and this time gets a response. Somewhere in her past she remembers hearing people talk about what to do when you are lost. You're supposed to stay put, but she doubts they have ever encountered the world she's in.

Footsteps approach from somewhere ahead and the whoosh of wind indicates someone, or something is coming fast. She's ready to dart in the other direction—wherever that is—when she hears a familiar voice. It's Renay. She has a glow around her like a strange aura, making her light up in the darkness. The light adds a warmth to Renay, helping to ease the tension in Jessica's body.

"Jessica? Am I glad I found you," she says, "Something is back there and it's chasing me. Hurry, we have to get out of here."

Jessica shakes her head. "I don't know where here is. I can't find the house or the talking stones or anything."

"Well, what do we do?" Renay asks.

Jessica shrugs. "Where's the mirror you came through?"

"Behind me, I guess, but we can't go back there, it's too dangerous. C'mon, let's go back the way you came in."

Jessica grabs Renay's hand, a gesture she has only repeated a few times in her life. She normally hates the feel of hands, because they cause her nerve endings to go on full alert, but something about Renay doesn't do that and this makes her happy.

"This way, maybe we can find the way to your mirror and get you home, or maybe we can find the house."

"Renay? I'm scared," Jessica says, pulling herself closer to Renay.

"I know, I am too, but we'll get through this together. Now, come on, let's find a way out."

Renay leads and Jessica stays close to her, letting her feel her way through the dark. A small gust of wind blows across Jessica, and she turns in that direction. A small beam of light catches her attention, and she points it out to Renay.

Renay nods to her. "Boy, I'm glad you tapped on the mirror to let me know you were here. I'd never have found you any other way."

"What do you mean? I never tapped on anything."

Renay stops and crouches to eye level with Jessica. "If you didn't do it, then who did?"

The thrumming sound Jessica heard before Renay got there returned, only louder this time and with more fury. Waves of energy roll around them, threatening to knock Renay and Jessica over. Renay stands, squeezing Jessica's hand tight. The noise rises to a loud hum and Jessica feels it as well as hears it. Like the vibration from a speaker.

"Renay? What's happening?" Jessica yells over the din of a freight train as the noise intensifies, hurting her ears.

She's on the verge of shutting down, letting whatever it is take over, but before she does, Renay is pulling her toward the small light ahead. She suddenly gets the sense something is coming and closing in on them. Jessica doesn't let go of Renay but catches a glimpse of what's behind them.

Wide yellow eyes stare at her and they are coming closer.

"Renay, run!" She turns back to concentrate on the light ahead.

Renay is nearly there but Jessica wonders if they'll make it in time. The thing in the darkness is so close. It makes no sound and even if it did, the noise all around them would probably drown it out. The light from the small opening is getting larger but she also feels the thing closing in, its hands reaching for her. Before it does though, she falls into the air of reality, away from the upside-down world and the vacuum of the mirror.

A black-clawed arm extends over her head and reaches for Renay. She screams as it slashes across her stomach. The other hand connects with Jessica's face, grazing the sharp tips across her skin. She cries out and falls forward, tumbling into Renay and tangling into a ball on the dirty mattress below. Renay is panting, her exhalations coming in quick gasps. Jessica is breathing heavily too and feels Renay shaking just as much as she is.

"That was close," Renay says, something akin to relief in her expression. Renay's stomach shows through the ripped shirt. It's red and bleeding slightly, as an angry welp rises on her skin. Renay winces as she rubs it gently, then extends a hand toward Jessica, rubbing the place on her face where the creature cut her.

"It looks like we didn't come away unscathed after all."

Jessica touches her face and winces.

"What was that thing?" Renay asks.

Jessica shrugs, the tension starting to leave her body, but it's short-lived, as worry builds on Renay's face.

"Where am I?"

Jessica points at the mattress and then upstairs. Realization dawns on Renay's face.

"This is where you live?"

A door clacks open from somewhere above. "You better keep it down. Don't make me come down there," Wanda yells, then the door closes again. Jessica stares at Renay and sees the fear build on her face.

TWELVE
RENAY GETS CAUGHT

Renay paces the room, then crouches by Jessica and whispers to her forcing the words the best she can, "I have to get out of here. Now, Jessica. If one of them comes down here, I'm done."

Her heart is beating so rapidly, it may jump from her chest while Renay moves back and forth. She sweeps the room for an escape route. She sees a small window above a table in the corner and wonders if it's possible she could get through it. It looks like the only avenue she has.

"Can you help me?" she pleads.

Jessica stands and starts for the steps toward the stairs.

"Yes, good idea, watch the door for me while I try to get the window open," Renay says.

Renay clears a few things from the workbench. They rattle even though she tries to gingerly move them, wincing with each torturous noise, then takes a quick peek behind her to make sure no one is coming.

Jessica is standing vigilant by the stairs.

The cut on her stomach is throbbing with heat but she feels no pain, only a burning below the skin. She ignores it and continues clearing the surface.

Renay hops on the table, sitting at first and checking to make sure it will hold her weight. The thing is a bit rickety, and she wonders if it will fall over once she stands on it. Renay checks the window, tugging against it. It doesn't budge. A small clasp sits in the middle and she turns it downward, cringing when it makes a louder-than-expected click. She wiggles it gently and feels the window give. It slides to the side with a screech and Renay grits her teeth, then stops for a second, letting out the held breath she's been keeping in.

She quickly surveys the room and sees Jessica standing there, looking back at her by the stairs.

Renay relaxes and pulls at the window again. This time it slides all the way open. A gust of cold air blows in, causing a shiver to run through her. A dog barks in the distance but otherwise it's quiet outside. She's thankful it's dark enough out there to conceal what she's doing.

Renay pushes herself up and grabs the outside frame of the small opening. She wriggles up to her hips and feels things get snugger. She turns to the side and with all her strength jerks herself through. The extra effort frees the window from its frame though, and it topples downward onto the table.

Renay holds her breath, as the window shatters against the workbench. She hears movement in the house and squawking.

Other voices join in, lower, belonging to men. It's time to leave, but before she goes, she looks through the window one last time., she sees Jessica is across the room, her downturned face is a map of no expression.

Renay figures most children would be worried but Jessica, she knows, isn't like most. There's no time to help her, though, even if every fiber of Renay's body wants to.

Renay runs for the alleyway behind the house. Sharp cold enters her skin, but mostly through her bare feet. She hugs herself to keep the cold at bay. Thankfully, she didn't take her jeans off before falling asleep at her mother's house.

Renay yelps when her foot hits a frozen puddle. Her teeth chatter from the incessant cold but she doesn't stop. If she did, someone might see her. Identify her at the source. Her only plan at this point is to get back to her apartment and wake the landlord next door. Something that could bring the police, but Renay doesn't care, at least she won't die from hypothermia.

The trek is not an easy one, as Renay strides as quickly as possible along the city streets, ignoring whoops from some of the locals. A few sits outside a bar on the corner of a not-so-nice neighborhood. Renay figures it can't be worse than walking through downtown Columbus, but she has no desire to compare the two. The men turn back to whatever they're doing when she ignores them. To them, she hopefully looks like any other street vagrant or lady of the night.

She turns to the main road. Route 52 dissects Portsmouth with a four-lane highway. It's normally very busy but being 03:00 AM or thereabouts, she sees no cars.

Renay runs across the road and continues onward toward her apartment on Summit Street. At this point, she's only halfway there. Renay's teeth start a fresh fury of chattering.

She hugs herself harder, trying to ignore the biting wind on her skin and the numbness in her feet. The heat from her middle is a small comfort from the cold, but a worry nags at her as her mind turns to infection.

She turns the corner and sees she's one block from her place. What will the landlord think? Shit, what will Maddy think when she wakes and finds Renay missing? All things to worry about later. For now, she needs warmth and antibiotics, probably. Maybe a tetanus shot?

Snow flurries begin to fall when Renay turns the corner onto Summit. A fresh wind hits her in the back like a sledgehammer, and she feels herself topple forward on shaky legs, as she reaches her landlord's place.

Maude, please be home.

As she ascends the steps, she notices Mister Whiskers, Maude's yellow tabby cat sitting in the window, staring wanly at the late-night visitor. He raises his back and stretches lazily, then saunters to the window where he rubs his head against the glass.

Renay runs up the steps to Maude's front porch, then turns her attention to the door and knocks as hard as she can. She hears Mister Whiskers meowing loudly behind the door like a dog warning its master of an intruder. The cat seems more dog-like anyway, the way it follows Maude around.

The light comes on above her and she hears the bolts releasing from the door. It swings inward and Renay feels a glorious blast of heat hit her face and torso. The sweet smell of perfumed strawberries invades her nose, and she momentarily thinks of her mom's house and the fragrant melting wax in the candles she uses. Mister Whiskers rubs against her lower leg, making a rhythmic path of graceful figure eights, and purring loudly.

Maude stands there in an old robe, her hair up in curlers.

"Renay? What on earth are you doing? It's three thirty in the morning," Maude says, looking down at Renay's feet. "Where are your shoes?"

"It's a long story. I forgot my key at my mom's house. May I please use your phone to call her?"

"Yes, of course. Come in before you die out there."

Renay walks into the pristine house.

Maude and Maddy are cut from the same cloth and whether Maude shows it or not, she's cringing at Renay's dirty socks touching the clean floor. "Sorry if I get mud on your floor. I didn't have time to get my shoes before I left the house I was in."

Maude shakes her head in obvious disapproval, staring at Renay's ripped shirt.

"I hope you know some boys are assholes. Pardon my bad language. You can do better than that."

Renay shrugs, shaking off the remainder of the cold, and goes to a stand on the other side of the room below the stairs. She's thankful to see a black phone there. Maude, and a few others—Maddy included—still had these relics plugged into their wall and she's grateful for it.

Renay sits in the old chair and Mister Whiskers jumps in her lap, trying to get her attention.

Maude picks him up. "Leave the girl alone you old lover boy. Come on, I'll get you a late-night snack." Maude leaves for the other room with the old cat purring like the reverberation of a car engine.

Renay calls her mother and waits for her to answer then instinctively touches her stomach, wincing from the pain this produces.

The fabric at the edge of the torn shirt is melted like it had been singed with a lighter.

The welts on her stomach throb with heat and she moves uneasily in her chair. This night had turned into an adventure she'd never forget, and Renay thinks it will stay on her mind for some time to come. But what can she do with it? That's the question. But most importantly, how can she help Jessica?

Thirteen
Jessica's Troubles

The door slams open at the top of the stairs and Jessica turns to see Wanda and Carl descending the steps. She grabs the small makeup case on the mattress and puts it in her pocket before they see it. The last thing she wants is for Wanda to know she had been digging in her personal stuff. The last time she messed with anything of Wanda's in the bathroom, she got a hand across her face.

"What the hell was that noise?" Carl yells out.

"It sounded like something broke down here," Wanda says.

Jessica is standing there in front of the workbench with shards of glass strewn around her feet and on the table behind her. She shakes partly from fear, but mostly from the wind gushing from the open window.

Carl steps around her and inspects the window and the table. "Did you do this? Were you trying to get out through there?" he says, looking at Jessica and pointing at the broken opening.

Jessica shakes her head and Wanda crouches in front of her. "Don't lie to us, girl. You know it won't go well. Who broke the window if you didn't?" Wanda studies her face. "Have you been hitting yourself again?"

"She obviously busted it, stupid," Carl says. "She can't talk, or have you forgotten?"

Wanda stands scowling and hangs her head, looking defeated, at least to Carl but her anger seems to be channeling in Jessica's direction. She grabs her wrist and yanks.

"Come on, little girl, I have the perfect place for you. Ain't no windows there," she says.

Carl shakes his head while scanning the area around the bench. "Just take her somewhere she can't cause any damage. I got an errand to run, and the guy upstairs can't be left waiting."

Wanda jerks Jessica forward, causing her to stumble onto her knees. The impact on the floor sends shockwaves through her and she can feel it all the way through her teeth.

Wanda pulls again and Jessica feels herself being elevated to her feet. She shuffles ahead, unable to maintain her balance with Wanda leading her.

Jessica falls one more time before reaching the steps, then Wanda practically drags her up on her butt. Every time Jessica tries to get her footing, Wanda knocks her off balance.

Once they reach the top, Wanda gives another tug on Jessica and sends her skidding onto her back. Jessica's body is screaming inside, and she wants to do the same, but can't. She opens her mouth wide and tries so hard to let it out, but grunts and moans are all she produces. Tears roll down her face and she bites her hand instead and hits her head against the floor. Anything to make the pain Wanda is inducing stop.

Wanda scoffs and releases Jessica's wrist.

She slams the basement door shut, then looks at Jessica. "I hear you. I think you can talk, but you're just fooling everyone. Well, it doesn't matter because you're going in the closet."

Jessica rolls to her belly and then gets to her hands and knees. She sees Wanda opening the small door to the storage area under the stairs. Jessica's mind goes to dark places, remembering what it's like under there. The darkness and the spiders crawling around in her hair. The last time she was in there, she left scratches in the paint on the door. She shakes her head violently, then turns to the living room—anywhere she can hide. Jessica crawls toward the other side of the couch and curls into a ball. She begins to rock frantically, putting her hand in front of her to focus, but it's not working. Everything inside her is a mess and she can't keep her heart from thumping wildly in her chest. She wants to run as far away as possible.

Claw screams and jumps from one end of his perch to the other. He flaps his wings even though he can't go anywhere due to the tether on his ankle.

"Get the girl! She's over here!"

The bird's warning makes Wanda run faster than usual. She grabs Jessica and pulls her to stand, then starts dragging her kicking and clawing toward the closet. Jessica extends her arm and grabs a wad of Wanda's hair, then pulls. A large chunk of filthy blond hair comes with the yank. Wanda screams but it doesn't stop her, and she renews her fight against Jessica, inching closer to the opening of the prison Jessica wants no part of.

"What the hell's going on out here," someone says.

Jessica turns her head to see a large man standing in the doorway to the kitchen. He's heavy-set with large arms. Tattoos cover them from top to bottom. Jessica can only make out a row of skulls on one of his forearms. He purses his lips like he doesn't care much for the situation.

"Hey, is it a good idea to damage the merchandise?"

"Wrong package, Bresnik," Carl says while walking from the door to the basement.

Bresnik nods and turns back to the kitchen. "As long as she's alive, I suppose," he says, paying little attention to Wanda.

Jessica pulls against Wanda one more time, but instead of knocking her foster mom off balance, Wanda steps sideways with more speed than Jessica thought she possessed. Wanda shoves Jessica into the closet, causing her to fall forward and hit her head on the wall inside.

Before Jessica can regain her footing, the door slams shut behind her and she hears it latch from the outside. Bolts, three in all, slide into place and Jessica feels the weight of each one. She isn't ready to stop though, and she kicks violently against the door with all the power she can muster.

"Good luck kicking that door down. It's solid wood," Wanda says from the other side.

Jessica stops for a second as dust particles fall around her, touching her skin and making her wince. They feel like barbs sticking into her. Her mind wanders to the spiders, and she renews the fury of self-abuse. Every fiber in her says fight and she explodes with anger, pounding on the door with her fists, her feet, and anything she can.

Her insides call out in agony and her skin crawls like the spiders and insects she's sure are all around her. If she gets the chance, she'll rip Wanda and Carl to shreds, pull their arms off, and feed one to the other.

Jessica stops for a moment, wondering where that thought came from, and feels the cut on her face throb with heat.

Jessica is in a darkened tunnel as fear falls over her mind and is absorbed by another feeling ... death. She doesn't understand why, but it's there and she can't shake it.

Jessica wants to hurt those who hurt her and oddly she feels at peace. The darkness may be a friend after all.

The morning light peeks over the gray horizon as Carl drives the car deliberately slow along Route 23, staying steady between the lanes of traffic. He settles in behind a car going around fifty miles per hour then sets the cruise control.

"Why so slow," Bresnik says.

"Because, my Albanian friend, we don't want the law pulling us over. They are thick through here and won't mind doing a quick search of the license plate. You know what they'd find?"

"No, but I'm sure it's no good."

"That's right. This car is stolen, my friend," Carl says. "If they find out, then they'll run both of us in, me for the car and you for the fact you're here illegally."

Bresnik shrugs. "I suppose. Do you think the girl is safe with your wife?"

"Yeah, she's good. Wanda gets mad and all and may rough her up, but she won't do anything else. Now that Jess is in the closet,

I figure Wanda is lounged back on the couch near passed out from the heroin she's injected in her veins."

"Doesn't give me much confidence," Bresnik says. "You know I need the girl alive. This whole thing won't work any other way."

"I know," Carl says. "Don't worry, I got you. The girl and the boy you found. I don't really understand why you need her, though."

"It's because she's, I don't know, special, I suppose," Bresnik says.

"Special? Like she's messed up in the head? That what you mean?"

"I assure you, Carl, that girl is not simple-minded. She sees things we can only imagine. I know this because I've witnessed occurrences I can't even begin to explain in the old country."

Carl laughs. "Like what?"

"Magic, my friend. Kids like her can summon things and keep them at bay as well. We'll need her as a catalyst of sorts when we encounter the monster we are up against," Bresnik says.

"I get it, the monster. Tell me, Bresnik, why do you think it will be different this time? What makes you think that thing will play nice?"

Bresnik smiles. "Because of the mirror."

"That old thing," Carl scoffs. "I put it in the girl's room like you told me to, but I don't get it. It doesn't look any different than any other I've seen."

"Appearances can be deceiving, my friend. That plain old mirror in your house is actually called The Mirror of Souls. I dug it up near the place where we last encountered the creature. It's magic and was the missing ingredient to controlling the monster. If I'd had it last time, we wouldn't have lost your child."

"I don't see how a mirror will change anything. What is that monster anyway."

"A fairy of sorts."

Carl chuckles, "Fairies? Like Tinkerbell?"

"Oh no, much more insidious. It's a changeling, actually placed there by fairies for the exchange of another child and it feeds on trauma and pain. The more the creature gets the better."

"Damn, Bresnik, you are crazier than I give you credit for," Carl says.

"Oh no, exchanges of children go way back and if you know how to use the magic, you can manipulate the changeling into doing what you want. That's why I wanted you to place the mirror in her room. The girl lost her mother at a young age, even before she knew of her, and that has to bring a lot of suffering with it. I figure she is a prime candidate for the monster's appetites."

Carl shakes his head, "I don't know where you come up with this shit, but if I didn't see the creature, I wouldn't believe any of it."

"Well, Carl, it's what you pay me for, among other things."

"Got it, like this kidnapping. You better be right about this one. Where is he, anyway?"

"He's in the Grove City area. In a small house a few blocks from the interstate," Bresnik says. He smiles. "Should be easy pickings since he lives there alone with his grandma."

"What's his name?" Carl asks.

Bresnik pulls out a file with some papers in it. The kind they keep in a records section at a school or hospital. He opens it and leans over for Carl to see. "His name is Trevor Reinhardt."

"How'd you pick him?"

"I don't know," Bresnik says. "It's like he fell into my lap."

FOURTEEN
BACK TO REALITY

The gray sky morning suits Renay's mood as she drives to work. The events of the weekend are still fresh in her mind. The strange encounter with the mirror and ending up in Jessica's basement was enough to make her question anything based on reality anymore.

The bus ride home to Columbus made her sad and long for her old life again. After she called her mom and explained the best she could why she was back in Portsmouth, blaming the whole experience on a night out with some friends. Maddy didn't understand how she could've left the house without her or Trevor knowing, and Renay didn't explain it any further.

Once she was back, she took Trevor to get pizza and see a movie, pretending like nothing had happened at all. The whole weekend she rubbed her stomach—something else Maddy knew nothing about—trying to ease the burning sensation the scar produced. Three long red marks lay across her skin, and she couldn't shake the sight of the shadow creature that nearly came from the mirror after her. Thankfully it retreated before appearing completely in the real world. The eyes, yellow and glowing, and the darkness of the form. It seemed to go on forever like a black hole in outer space.

Renay shivers from the thought of the phantom, sending through her a cold she can't seem to shake. Even the heater in the car doesn't help to make her comfortable.

The whole incident seems like a dream or maybe a nightmare. She has an appointment with Jessica this morning. It should be interesting given what they've been through recently, but Renay feels they can make it work. At least she knows inside the mirror they can.

Renay opens the door to the clinic and scans the waiting room but doesn't see Jessica anywhere in sight. She turns to the window between the reception desk and the waiting room. Ruby stands inside, looking over the planner and jotting down schedules.

"Hey, Ruby. Where's Jessica this morning? Isn't she my first patient?"

Ruby looks up from the planner. "She's not here? I honestly never noticed. Do you want me to call? I mean, it's not likely they'll answer. Most with burner phones don't unless they recognize the number. I'd say even if Carl and Wanda did, they'd ignore it. Those two have their own schedule."

Renay shakes her head. "No, I'll wait. When's my next appointment?"

Ruby runs her finger along the list on the planner and stops on a name. "Looks like Sally, the little girl from across town. The one with the nice family."

"Thanks," Renay says. Nice family? Renay thinks about Jessica and how she must feel with her not-so-nice family. She hopes Jessica is doing well but something inside her feels this isn't the case. Renay opens the door to the gym and disappears inside.

The day is nearly over. A long one, seeing a range of different kids with various diagnoses. Renay notices Jonathan has removed the mirror in the treatment room after the first encounter she and Jessica had. Renay couldn't blame the man. The disruptive manner of the encounter made it hard for him to leave anything to chance.

Renay nearly makes it out the front door when she sees Trish and Brenda coming from the gym.

"Hey, girl, you feeling better," Trish says.

"Yeah, you weren't looking good the other day," Brenda adds.

Renay shrugs. "I am," she says and rubs her stomach over the fabric of her shirt. The pain of the slash has subsided, but it's still irritated like a rash that won't go away. "I think I need more rest."

Trish smiles. "Sounds like a plan. Maybe soon we can all get together for drinks or something. I know some people, maybe a fella I'd like for you to meet."

Renay shudders at the thought of a hook-up. The memory of Mike and the blood comes back to her, then losing Molly. It's too much. Even though it's been a year or so, she isn't ready to meet anyone. "Sure, drinks sound good. Maybe when, like you said, I settle in a little more."

"Absolutely," Trish says. "Take your time, only when you're ready. "Trish and Brenda leave through the front door, giggling as they go. Renay wishes she could be that carefree, but for her, the pain is so ingrained, she can think of nothing else. She wants so badly to be back with Trevor and her mom.

It won't be long.

Small flecks of snow are falling outside and the tree in the corner flashes its lights in time with the falling particles. Renay sighs.

Possibilities are presenting themselves but is she ready? Only one way to find out. If only she had a crystal ball or magic mirror.

The latter makes her laugh.

Fifteen
Renay's Discovery

After Renay pulls from the parking lot, she thinks of going by Jessica's house but changes her mind, afraid Carl or Wanda might recognize her. She decides to go home instead and see what she can find on her computer.

The darkened sky is depressing as she ascends the steps to her rental. Mr. Whiskers greets her at the door, purring and meowing while rubbing the bottom of her pants.

"Better get home, lover boy, Maude will be looking for you."

He doesn't relent and she has to push him away. Mr. Whiskers seems to get the message and saunters along, jumping onto the railing and then onto Maude's porch.

Renay unlocks the door and lets it swing inward to the empty, silent house and she's faced with a sense of loneliness but at least peace. Renay drops her bag by the couch, switches the light on, and pulls her computer out.

After placing it on the coffee table, she disappears into the kitchen and goes to the refrigerator. A few beers sit on the top shelf, and she figures it should be enough to help get the juices flowing.

Renay grabs one and heads back to the living room and gets comfortable while turning on the computer. Taking a drink, Renay thinks about what to put in the search bar.

She starts with Jessica's name first but gets no hits. Renay thinks it's because she's a foster kid and her name is protected, so she types in Carl and Wanda next. Lots of different people come up but as she scrolls, she sees an article with Carl and Wanda she's looking for mentioned.

Renay clicks on it and reads. The article was from a few years ago and the newspaper came from Kentucky where the incident occurred.

It was a report about a missing child; Wanda and Carl's son. The two were found in a field, left there by a man neither one knew. They said he was a foreigner and may have been a terrorist.

It all seems strange to her, the fact they were out of state, and they may have been kidnapped? So many things are not adding up. The missing child would explain why they have a foster kid but why did the child go missing in the first place and who was this guy, a foreigner?

Renay decides to start down a rabbit hole and check for other children who had gone missing in the same area. What she finds is shocking. Quite a few have disappeared from various ages and around the area in general, girls not much younger than her but mostly in the Southern Ohio region. The cases seem to have no connection to what Renay is looking for.

She continues to search and finds a historical article about an old cemetery near where Wanda and Carl were found, and when she sees the picture, Renay gasps. It's the same one she saw by the upside-down house.

Renay clicks on another article, this one about the area where the gravestones are located and sees a house sitting next to them.

The picture is old and sepia-toned, making it hard to distinguish in the newspaper article, but she's almost positive it's the same house.

This one has a small shed beside it with a sign. It looks like Glasshut but it's hard to make out. It must be where he made the mirrors.

She continues to read. Dubbed by locals as the Mirror House, it belonged to a German glass maker who specialized in, Renay can't believe it, mirrors. They adorn the walls and the memory of looking into them stands out in Renay's mind, sending chills all over her body. The story says the man took his life after his wife and child were killed by locals for the crimes against the church although it didn't specify.

As scary as that is, another article makes her shudder even more. Apparently, children had gone missing there in the past and it led historians to think the gravestones marked their burial site.

There, near the bottom of the article, she also sees words written in German. *Der Spiegel meiner Seele*, translated in the article to be "The Mirror to my Soul". She also sees the translation for the shed. It's Glasshutte or Glassworks.

Renay doesn't know what to make of it and the whole thing spooks her. The sense she will have a hard time sleeping tonight comes over her as she continues to read.

The historical article is connected to another one about the house burning down.

She clicks on the article and sees it's also about missing children. Renay didn't expect that, and her curiosity is heightened as she continues to read.

The story is called, ""The Missing Children of the Field"", and a picture of the old house and gravestones is featured prominently beside it, then another with the house a pile of ashes.

In the article, it mentions the house was an orphanage of sorts with a local woman serving as a nanny. According to the newspaper piece, the house burned but there were no bodies inside, prompting the authorities to think the children and the nanny went missing before the incident occurred.

Rumors were that several children found possible demise at the hands of some unknown killer, one who may have been lurking in the shadows the whole time, then burned the house down before escaping.

All that was left of the house was a sole mirror which they buried in the same grave with the glass maker and his wife and child.

It remains one of the greatest mysteries of the area and is unsolved even today. *How does it all connect?* Renay asks herself but can find no ready answers. This is getting her nowhere and she decides to shut the computer down.

The house is dark, and she rubs her eyes and sets the laptop to the side, yawning, then stretching, thinking bed might be a good idea.

She stands and hears whispers float in the air from the other room followed by a loud thump. Her stomach warms and she is suddenly very uncomfortable. Renay's heart speeds up and she trembles, breathing heavily.

Her midsection is throbbing and shooting pain as another noise fills her ears. This time, it's a tapping sound and it's not coming from the next room but the mirror on the wall.

Fresh shivers run through her as she thinks of the incident in her mom's house.

Renay reaches for the lamp but before she can, another sound permeates her ears, grating on her nerves. Claws scratch the wood and Renay freezes in place. The blood drains from her face and her veins turn to ice as her heart thumps so hard she's afraid it will jump from her chest.

Yellow eyes fill the void in the darkened room and Renay's legs go rubbery. The eyes, cat-like and thinning, concentrate on her, sizing her up for the kill. Renay steps slowly backward, away from the eyes, but watches as they appear to come closer.

They hover in the empty air like they've fallen away from the mirror. Renay turns and runs for the stairs, but a pain shoots through her middle and she falls onto the first step, hitting her chin.

Coppery-tasting fluid fills her mouth as sharp pain goes through her teeth and tongue. The room spins for a moment, and she turns her head, sure the eyes and whatever is attached to them will be on her, but she sees nothing.

Renay sits up and feels as though she will pass out, but she manages to keep her composure, at least for now. Her midsection continues to throb, and deep dread fills her mind. Is she safe? Is Jessica in trouble? The thoughts take over everything she's thinking.

Across town, Jessica's mind is on the burning in her jaw. She has stopped hitting and biting herself but the irritation from the scar the creature gave her is becoming increasingly painful.

She tries to ignore it, but the nagging discomfort is taking over. Something moves in her pocket, and she fishes around for the offending item, pulling out the makeup mirror she used to go into the upside-down world last time.

A light glints from it, exposing her reflection in the total darkness. She concentrates on it, hoping to go inside once again, but is distracted by movement.

A shadow darts from side to side, moving rapidly as Jessica holds the makeup case tighter. It hesitates and then moves toward her until it consumes the whole face of the mirror.

The opening turns yellow and an eye with a black line in the middle stares back at her. The line blinks a few times like it's studying her. Jessica's breath quickens and she snaps the lid close and throws the compact away.

The sound of breaking glass fills her ears.

The scar on her face eases and she lowers herself to the floor. She whimpers and rocks back and forth with her breath coming in quick succession for a moment before she calms.

Jessica wants out of this place but realizes that won't happen anytime soon. Shuffling feet go by outside the door, stopping in front of the opening. Jessica's anticipation heightens at the thought the door may open but is deflated when the footsteps go away.

Her world turns to the desperation she felt when Wanda put her in here and with no mirror, there is no escape.

Sixteen
The Mirror Trap

The door swings open with such force, it bangs against the staircase loudly. Light fills the doorway, bright and painful after spending hours, maybe even days locked in the dark. Jessica squints, trying to adjust her vision to the sudden change. She crawls out of the space and looks toward the window.

Night had already fallen by now. When she slowly gets to her feet, Jessica also notices a small plastic Christmas tree on the stand next to the couch. It's surprising to her Wanda would even think to put one up.

Wanda grabs Jessica's arm and yanks her onto her feet, clearly annoyed that she is taking so long.

"Get your ass moving. I'm not going to drag you to your room," Wanda says.

Jessica complies but moves slowly, her legs being numb from being cramped up in that dark hole.

Claw is jumping furiously as usual on his perch, snapping his beak, and blurting out, "Go to your room!" over and over.

When Jessica gets there, she steps inside, and Wanda slams the door behind her. The room is plunged into darkness except for the small amount of light coming from the window produced by the streetlamp outside.

Even though Jessica knows Wanda is doing it out of anger, she likes the calmness of the shadows in her room. The space is larger than the closet so she can stretch and feel much more comfortable. The bite marks on her arms throb and her face is red hot from the lashing she gave it, but she ignores the pain and instead concentrates on the one place she wants to go. To escape where she lives.

She's done with Wanda and Carl. Through with all of them.

This time, when she returns to the upside-down place, she feels she'll find the children again because she's entering through the mirror in her room.

Jessica kneels in front of it and sees her reflection in the dim light. Her hair is messy, and her face is a mask of shadows and red marks that suit her mood. She touches the glass in front of her and feels the cold, smooth texture. It invigorates her and she concentrates on the edge near the frame.

There she sees it, the stretching lines, where the real world and the upside-down world meet. Her mind goes there and a gentle tug on her body commences. A second later, she's in the mirror.

Jessica stands and looks wanly into the darkened corridor of gray and black waves of energy, flowing out into the distance.

They call to her and coax her into a feeling of relaxation and calm. Noise comes from the void. It's a low hum at first, then the sounds become words. The children are speaking to her, calling her to join them. Jessica smiles and walks into the abyss beyond. Soon, she sees the house in the field, sitting in its usual spot and upside-down position.

The stones are glowing, a visible and surprising change from their usual dormant state. The light reflects off the mirrors of the house and she sees images in each one. All of the other children were close to her age.

Some have strange clothing like they belong in an old-time picture. The ones she's seen in books and movies.

Come see us, Jessica, come play, please.

Jessica moves toward the house slowly and steps onto the porch, feeling the slight flutter in her stomach she expects when the house turns right side up.

We are the mirror of your soul, Jessica, and we love you with all our hearts.

Jessica isn't sure what that means but she is encouraged and intrigued to go to them.

The children keep calling to her and she steps closer, and her mind is calmer and clearer than ever before. The feeling is wonderful. No busy thoughts or nerves that won't stop prodding her and making her mad. No hitting herself to make it go away.

This is the way she's always wanted to be, as normal as everyone else.

———◆◇◆———

Carl pulls the car to stop in an alley not far from the house they plan to break into. It's early morning and the two have spent the last couple of days planning how this would go. Carl had driven by the house several times in the past two days, careful to keep from being detected. An alley behind the house looks to be the best option to enter the property. The plan is to run in, club the old woman, and take the kid. Easy as that. The way they'd planned it.

Carl takes a deep breath as he prepares himself for the job ahead.

"The whole operation will be over in less than fifteen minutes, twenty at most," Bresnik says.

Carl nods. "Let's be wary of cameras, okay? This is Columbus and I'm sure they're mounted on every corner, even in the residential areas."

"Don't worry, it's why we wear hats," Bresnik says and hands a black ballcap to Carl.

Carl puts the cap on. He pulls it down tight.

"Now, as an extra layer of protection, I have these," Bresnik says. He pulls out two black surgical masks from his coat pocket.

"Aw, hell no, I ain't wearing one of those. I didn't get that damned vaccine and I ain't putting on a mask either," Carl protests.

"Come on, my friend, I know all that stuff was bullshit, but you have to admit, it would be a great way to cover up our faces just in case a camera does see us. I found them at a drugstore dirt cheap and figured they may come in handy."

Carl takes one of them, considers it, then smirks. "Whatever, I guess it can't hurt to wear one to cover our faces. This thing is coming off as soon as we get back to the car."

Bresnik smiles. "That's the spirit."

"You got the club?"

"Right here, Carl," Bresnik says. "I won't hit her too hard, just enough to put her out."

"I don't give a shit if you kill her, but do it quickly," Carl says.

"Nah, I won't kill the old girl. I'll just make her wish she was dead."

Carl opens his door and steps out onto the pavement. Bresnik follows and they make their way slowly through the alleyway. In seconds, they are at the back door, where they use a crowbar to break the lock. No alarms go off. No dogs bark either.

They make their way upstairs and hear what they want to avoid.

"Who are you?" the woman calls out, then they see her reaching for the phone on the wall. Before she can pick up the receiver, Bresnik thumps her on the back of the head.

The phone falls to the floor with a crack, and the woman crumbles beside it with blood pouring from the back of her head.

"Damn, did you kill her?" Carl asks.

"Naw, she'll be fine. I told you I'd make her wish she was dead. When she wakes, she'll have one hell of a headache," Bresnik says, laughing.

They both turn suddenly to see a boy standing in a doorway off the hall. He rubs his eyes and looks at them both wanly.

"Grandma? Is that you making all the noise?"

Carl nods to Bresnik and the Albanian man moves toward the boy.

"Hey, Trevor. Your grandma is sleeping and now we're going to take over."

Trevor looks at the floor where his Grandma Maddy is lying, then back to the men with the masks on and his eyes widen.

He turns to run but Bresnik has him before he takes one step. "Got you," he says, wrapping his big arms around Trevor.

The boy kicks and screams but it does no good. Carl hands Bresnik a handkerchief.

"Here, gag him with this."

Bresnick takes the rolled cloth and stuffs one end in Trevor's mouth, wraps it around his head, and ties it in the back. He then produces some plastic zip ties. Bresnik secures Trevor's hands and feet with them and throws the boy over his massive shoulder.

"Seems a bit harsh don't you think?" Carl asks as the boy struggles with tears in his eyes.

"Naw, better than him hurting himself," Bresnik says.

Bresnik heads for the stairs and Carl follows. They run from the house toward their vehicle parked in the alley.

Once in the car, Bresnik secures Trevor with the seatbelt, then gets in the passenger side. "Let's go."

Carl pays no attention but steps on the accelerator. They bark tires as they leave.

"You think it will go alright now?" Carl asks.

"Yes, all is as planned. Just like last time. Quit worrying. Your son will be returned to you. The curse works that way. This thing we're dealing with has been around for a long time, my friend. The people in the old country know it well, although some have forgotten. It takes the child and returns it better as long as you have another to give. But remember, we have to have the girl."

"Alright, I got it. Let's get the hell out of here."

Part Two

Away with us he's going
The solemn eyed
For he comes, the human child
To the waters and the wild
With a faery, hand in hand,
From a world more full of weeping than he can understand
From The Stolen Child,
W. B. Yeats, 1889

Seventeen
Abduction

The clinic is abuzz with activity when she arrives. Renay's caseload has five patients for the day, but as she looks at it, she notices one missing—Jessica. It had been a few days since she saw the girl in the basement and it's starting to worry her. Renay goes to the office when she gets a break and lets Ruby know she's going to call Jessica's parents.

"Good luck," she says, "Last time we had to call Child Protective Services."

The phone rang several times before going to nothing. No voicemail, so Renay assumes it's not a cell she's calling. She's making too many assumptions because she knows deep down Jessica is in trouble. It's the only outcome she can fathom. Renay hangs up the phone and shakes her head.

"No one home?" Ruby asks.

"I suppose not," Renay says. "How long have they gone with missing appointments in the past," Renay asks.

"Oh, honey, let me tell you, we've called those people in before, more than once," Ruby says. "Always the same result too. They go over there and check things out, say it's okay, and next thing you know, she's back here. It's like a merry-go-round."

Renay nods. "Well, I'm worried about her, maybe call CPS again?"

"Alright, I'll give them a call now."

"Thanks, Ruby," Renay says, then returns to the gym. The light hum of the instrumental Christmas tunes fills her ears for a second until they are drowned out by the noise of children playing in the gym.

Jonathan is in the corner getting her next client started and she is momentarily distracted with things.

After the client's session, Renay returns him to his waiting parents up front, then turns to Ruby. "Any word?"

"Oh, plenty," she says. "I called CPS, and they said they had sent people over there this morning, but no one was home. They're checking with other family of Wanda's in the area. They hope to have more information shortly. I don't know, they may have gone on a drug run or something."

Renay thinks about it, then considers paying a visit over there this evening. At least drive by. She starts to turn to the gym again when the phone rings. Ruby answers and nods a few times, then she turns pale.

"Yes, she's right here, I'll give the phone to her now," she says, then hands the receiver to Renay. "I'm sorry."

Renay takes the phone and slowly brings it to her ear. "Yes, this is Renay Reinhardt, who am I speaking to?"

The voice on the other end sounds methodical like every word is being chosen carefully. "This is Nurse Hutchins at Grant Hospital, and we have your mother. She's unconscious at the moment but we need you to come as quickly as possible."

The words congeal in Renay's brain and the world tilts. "W-w-what happened? Did she fall? What about my son? Do you have him there too?"

There's silence on the other end for a second before the nurse responds with a solemn, uncertain, "Well ... your son has been abducted. It was an apparent break-in. The detective is here if you'd like to speak to her."

Ruby comes around the barrier to the office area and puts an arm around Renay.

Renay doesn't want it, but the stun is too great for her to protest. "Yes ... sure, I'll talk to her." Or rather, she thinks she said it.

After she heard "abducted", Renay's brain and body weren't communicating anymore.

Her fear was so great at that very moment, she could taste metal. *Abducted?* Of course, it was every parent's worst nightmare, but Renay firmly believed those things only happened to other people. *Have I not lost enough?*

"Here's Detective Fertig."

Renay hears beeping noises and the sound of muffled voices in the background while she waits for the detective. This is more than she can take. "Hi, Renay, this is Detective Christina Fertig with the Columbus Special Victims Unit," a very matter-of-fact female voice says.

"Special Victims? Has my son been hurt?" Renay's voice cracks as she tries to fight back the tears.

"No, not that we are aware of. At seven thirty this morning, two men broke into your mother's house in Grove City. We have reason to believe they had been preparing for this as there were no fingerprints and they only took your son. It seems like abduction was their motive.

"Your mother must have attempted to stop them because we found no blood other than hers at the scene. She's being well cared for here at the hospital. I'm sure they'll need to see you soon. We can talk more when you get here.

"We must get ahead of this, Renay. The first forty-eight hours are the most crucial in an abduction case."

"Are you sending anyone out to look for him? It's nine-fifty. They could be two or three states away by now."

"Yes, we have law enforcement looking for anything suspicious along all of the main highways coming out of Columbus. We'll send out an Amber Alert as well once we have a description of the car. A camera caught something outside on the street and we have people checking. I should know something within the hour, and we can send it out. We need as many eyes as we have on this. I look forward to meeting with you," Christina says.

"Okay, yes, I, I'll be there as soon as possible," Renay says. The call ends and all she can do is to stare at the receiver. How?

How did this happen? *Why* is this happening? Unable to come up with any answers, she sets the receiver back in its place and finally notices Jonathan by Ruby.

"Don't worry about anything here, just go. Get to your mom. Let us know what you find out when you get the chance."

Renay nods. She's having an out-of-body experience at the moment and can't seem to bring her thoughts together.

"Maybe someone should drive her?" Ruby says as she begins to turn from the reception desk. "An Uber?"

Renay shakes her head in response. She needed her car now more than ever. She goes through the gym and into the office.

Trish says something she doesn't hear, and Brenda pats her arm, but she doesn't feel any of it. It's all dreamlike at this point and even though she needs to be quick about getting out of there, she feels like she's wading through molasses.

The lights from the small tree in the corner flash off and on. She thinks of Trevor and how excited he is for Christmas.

God, if you're listening, please let me get my boy back in one piece. Don't take him away from me too.

Renay opens the car door and climbs inside just as the Amber Alert comes over her phone.

Eighteen
Revelations

On the way to the hospital, tears roll down her cheeks and sharp pains stab her chest.

What if she never sees him again? She wills that thought away but it's still at the surface. Another thought comes to her instead. One of a little girl who never got to be. Renay rubs her stomach like she had when Molly was still in there, growing. The same way she did with Trevor. A burning sensation takes over her middle, hot and angry, throbbing with pain.

Fresh tears roll down her face and her breath hitches as an uncontrollable torrent of grief wracks her body. She drives faster, not even realizing she's way over the speed limit until she passes a cop. Renay checks her rearview mirror as the car pulls out. No, they can't pull her over, not now. She slows a little as a car with Pikcton Police written on the side gets closer. Its lights come on and Renay utters a small curse, but instead of pulling in behind her, it speeds past for another car ahead.

Renay releases the breath she's holding and tries to control the crying, but she can't.

No amount of distraction will take it away.

Molly was gone way too soon and now Trevor was missing. She wails and hits the steering wheel repeatedly.

"Please, God, not my baby," she screams. "You took one, why are you taking the other?" Another Amber Alert comes over her phone. At least the police were trying but it gives her little relief.

When she arrives at Grant Hospital, she parks and gets out of the car as quickly as possible, trying to dry her tears, but failing to keep them at bay. She walks through the sliding glass door of the hospital and her phone rings. She looks to see the clinic number on the screen. Renay answers the phone and hears Jonathan on the other end.

"Renay. This is Jonathan. I saw the Amber Alert and I may know something about the car Trevor is in. I think it belongs to Carl and Wanda."

Renay's blood turns cold. "Thank you, Jonathan. I'll make sure and tell the detectives. Do you think Jessica is with them?"

"Who knows, but I'd assume so. I figure anything's possible at this stage," he says.

"Thanks. I appreciate everything. I'll keep you posted," Renay says.

"Sure thing. If you need anything make sure you call," Jonathan says, then hangs up the phone.

Renay walks to the receptionist at the front desk and asks for the room of Madeline Reinhardt. She's still in a daze and has no idea how she ended up on the third floor.

Still, by the time she finds the nurse's station, she's quickly directed to her mom's room. As she walks in, the sight of her mother is enough to send chills through her system. Wires and leads are connected to her, an IV is in her arm. Renay takes in the scene, watching the slow drip of fluid making its way into her mom's veins, and hears the monitor keeping time with Maddy's heartbeat.

Tears well in her eyes. "Oh, Mom, I'm sorry I wasn't there."

"Hello? Renay?" Someone says from behind her.

Renay turns to see two people standing there. One wears scrubs, the other is in a pantsuit with a badge displayed on her belt.

The nurse moves past Renay to check on her mother. Meanwhile, the detective extends a hand to Renay.

"I'm Detective Christina Fertig. We spoke on the phone earlier."

All Renay could do was nod.

"I think we may have a lead or two, but I'd like to get some more information on your son, if you don't mind."

"I may know who took him. I don't know where they went but I suspect I know who it is."

Christina's brow furrows before she pulls a small writing pad from her pocket inside her jacket and opens it. She takes a pen from her pocket as well. "What do you have?"

"The foster parents of one of my pediatric clients. My employer called after hearing the Amber Alert and identified the car as theirs," Renay explains.

Christina writes down the information. "Okay, what is your employer's name, we'll need to talk to them."

"It's Jonathan Burton. If you call the Carskills Rehab Clinic in Portsmouth, Ohio you can speak to him. I have a feeling they took my son because of my connection with Jessica, their foster daughter."

Christina continues to write. "What is your connection to the girl other than your work with her? Therapy, right?"

"Yes, I'm her Occupational Therapist. There was an incident at the clinic about two weeks ago. Jessica and I were working, and we both fell into a stupor. We passed out at the same time. The family was upset and took her out of the clinic, vowing not to return. Jonathan told me they are confrontational and not to worry about it, but I have a feeling they've done something to Jess and my son in retaliation. Don't ask me how I know, I just know," Renay says.

Christina looks up from her pad and studies Renay. "I'm sure you're telling me the truth, but it seems like there is more to the story. Some details you left out. Am I right?"

Renay breathes in and lets out a small sigh. "I have nothing else. I need to see my mom now. If I think of anything, I'll let you know."

The detective lowers her pad, then puts it back in her pocket along with the pen. "Any information is vital at this point. If you leave anything out, our chances of finding Trevor are much lower."

"There's nothing else," Renay says, her tone firmer this time.

The detective nods slowly, a shred of doubt shines brightly in her eyes.

"Alright then. We'll head down to Portsmouth to investigate the home of the foster parents and get as much information as possible. What time does the rehab clinic close?"

"At five, usually, but Jonathan tends to stick around longer, finishing up paperwork," Renay says.

"We'll get right on it," Christina says. "Please don't hesitate to call if any other details come to mind."

"I will," Renay says.

Christina turns to leave. Renay watches as she goes through the door and talks to a couple of uniformed police officers in the hall. She then leaves with one of them following behind her. The other stays on sentry detail outside the room. Renay sits by her mom's bed.

The nurse on duty looks at her. "I'm Nurse Hutchins, the one you talked to on the phone. Your mom is resting. I gave her some medicine to help with the pain. Is there anything I can get *you* before I leave?"

"No, thank you," Renay whispers as she reaches out to take her mother's hand.

"In that case, I'll leave you two alone."

Once the nurse leaves, Renay leans her forehead on the bed, her hand clasping her mother's. "Mom? I don't know if you can hear me, but I'm so sorry. I should have been there, I should have looked after you and Trevor." She sniffs, the fresh tears coming whether she wants them to or not. "I think I know who has Trevor, but ... Oh, Mom, you'll think I'm crazy." Renay decides to come clean, to tell her mother about the mirror, about Jessica, about the strange upside-down house and the yellow-eyed shadow. "I think, maybe, that's how I'm going to find Trevor. Don't ask me how I know, Mom. I just do." With that, she sits upright and pats her mother's hand. It's cold and strikes her as lifeless but she can't think that way. This is going to resolve itself the only way it can and the people who did this to her will pay.

Renay stands and walks to the door. She sees the officer outside talking to one of the nurses, a young girl, but the officer himself couldn't be much older. Renay slips past him as he keeps talking to the girl and heads for the elevator.

Moments later, she is in the lobby and going out the door of Grant Hospital. Next destination, Maddy Reinhardt's house.

NINETEEN
BACK TO THE UNKNOWN

Renay arrives at her mom's house in a few minutes. She gets out of her car and looks up to the second story. This house has scars now, too many for it to ever be the same again. The mirror that may lead her to Jessica, and hopefully Trevor, sits waiting for her arrival.

With determined, long strides, Renay makes her way onto the porch, ducking under the police tape. The wind picks up and blows her hood off, exposing the skin on her neck. Renay shivers, trying to get the keys out of her purse. Her fingers tremble as she fumbles the key into the lock. The deadbolt clicks open, and Renay pushes the latch on the large brass handle then enters the house. The door swings inside, creaking slightly, the sound echoing through the empty house.

Everything is just the same as it was a few days ago when she was here. The tree is lit in the corner, flashing every few seconds on cue. There were no decorations on the porch. Apparently, Maddy hadn't got there yet, and it didn't look like she would either. Renay could only hope now that her mom would even get back before Christmas. She's sure the road to recovery will be a long one.

Cold air blows from the hallway by the stairs leading to the kitchen. Renay peeks in and sees the back door is ajar. A broken piece of police tape blows in through the opening like a yellow flag of caution. The doorjamb is shattered, and Renay imagines the man who kicked it in, with Carl's angry tirades and sneering face firmly at the front of the thought.

She turns her attention to the task at hand and leaves the kitchen for the stairway, disappearing upstairs.

Blood stains the carpet midway down the hall, the place where she assumes her mother was assaulted. Tears moisten her eyes, but she chokes back her emotion.

She walks past it and stops at her room, then takes a deep breath before entering.

Inside, the room looks the same and untouched as the perpetrators must have found what they were looking for before the need to ransack the house. The mirror is on the chest of drawers all but calling for her to enter.

Renay remembers not long ago when she was only a teen in here listening to Audioslave on the Blitz radio station out of Columbus. So many distant memories and her life has taken some twists and turns, but she wants to think she's stronger because of them. Strong enough to find her son and Jessica.

Renay eases up to the dresser and pushes with her arms, then she turns to sit with her back to the mirror. She has no idea if this will work again. The last time Jessica called to her, but this time she's on her own. "Okay Jessica, you better be there," she says out loud to the empty room. The door to the room slams open, hitting the wall, as a wind howls through. Papers fly around the interior, caught in the throes of some vortex.

The wind picks up her hair and blows it around wildly on her head and into her eyes, at the same time electricity seems to build in the air, prickling her skin. Renay shakes her head trying to see past her tresses before a sudden shove against her chest leaves her breathless. The scar on her stomach throbs with fire as if signaling something dangerous on the horizon. Before she could wrap her head around the sensations, tendrils of black threads wrap around her middle, pulling her backward.

This is different than any time before and Renay has no time to register anything as she's dragged into the mirror behind her.

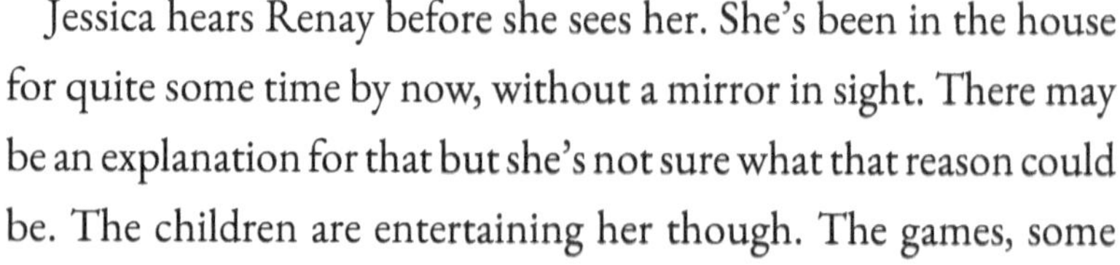

Jessica hears Renay before she sees her. She's been in the house for quite some time by now, without a mirror in sight. There may be an explanation for that but she's not sure what that reason could be. The children are entertaining her though. The games, some with old-looking marbles and dice, are strange to Jessica, but she's thrilled to be part of them.

The center of the house is full of activity, more than before. The nanny has brought even more kids in, coming from other rooms in the house. They can't speak to her, and she feels it's a strange thing as she can't talk outside the mirror, but they can't talk in here. Jessica points to things to convey her intent, and they seem to understand, most of the time.

So many things in this world are odd to Jessica and she takes advantage of some of them, like her ability to walk on the ceiling. She found this out by accident when one of the children threw a paper airplane and it caught on a shelf near the top of the room.

Jessica stretched her arms to reach for it, but she wasn't tall enough to retrieve it, then suddenly, she had it in her grasp. When she looked down, she saw herself halfway up the wall!

Since then, she had been walking all over the house, top and bottom. Another thing she found was the ability to go through one mirror in the house and end up coming out of another somewhere else.

The children couldn't do this, so it made it easy for her to find their hiding places, making her the clear winner of hide-and-seek games. The bent reality here is so much better than the real world Jessica lives in, and she never wants to leave. Not anymore.

Jessica hears Renay again, distracting her from the fun she's having. Renay sounds like she is in trouble, like she's lost. Her calls are incessant and Jessica frowns, regarding the children, as they seem to be pleading for her to stay. She shakes her head.

"I'll be back, I promise," she says and rushes out into the yard. Behind her, the house turns in the wrong direction again, but she doesn't look back, only picks up speed, heading into the field and the dark beyond.

Twenty

The Investigation Starts

Two Portsmouth Police cars were parked outside when Detective Fertig arrives at the Burns' house. Another unmarked vehicle is parked on the other side of the street.

Detective Ben Young, an old friend of hers is standing beside it and motions her to that side. The letters PPD glow on his jacket from the light of the headlights, as Christina pulls her sport utility vehicle in front of Ben's car. She parks the truck and gets out.

Ben had followed up on the lead Renay gave her and visited the clinic where she works. He talked with Jonathan Burton, the owner of the business, and he had some not-so-nice things to say about Carl and Wanda Burns. They rarely showed up with Jessica for appointments and weren't the most congenial couple you'd meet.

Christina wonders how they stayed under the radar of the local services in this area. The problem was they still had so little to go on. How were these two connected to Trevor's disappearance was the real question and she had no answers. The Burns' car was missing as well. Renay sounded so convinced over the phone. It saddened Christina to think this may be a dead end.

"What have we got?" she asks, as she steps up to Ben.

"We've secured the perimeter and haven't seen any lights on inside. Someone's in there though, because we can hear screaming from the front room. Someone with a shrill voice is telling us to stay away. Yelling he or she doesn't allow cops inside. I thought about breaking the door down but wanted to wait until you arrived," Ben replies.

"You did good. Nothing against your guys over there, but I want the inside of the house to remain as intact as possible," she says,

"Now, let's go and I dare that fucker to try anything."

Christina takes the lead with Ben following. They go to the front steps of the place and Christina turns to the uniformed officers. "One of you go to the back in case they try to run to the alley."

One of the cops nods and disappears into the driveway on the side of the house, his gun extended in front of him and a flashlight next to it. Christina motions for Ben and the other officer to follow her up the steps. She takes one side of the door and Ben the other. They lean against the wood facing the entrance door and Christina calls out to whoever is inside.

"I'm Detective Christina Fertig of the Columbus Police Department and we have this house secured. We need you to come to the door so we can talk to you. If you fail to comply, we have no choice but to bust the door down."

A voice, shrill and loud screams back its response. "Go away, no cops!"

Christina looks at Ben and he shrugs. "Same as before," he says.

"Is the door locked?" Christina asks.

"I don't think so."

Christina reaches slowly to the handle and depresses the button on top. The door clicks and swings inward. "On my lead," she says then steps inside, extending her gun in front of her body. "We're inside, don't do anything stupid. We only want to talk to you," she says.

The room ahead is dark except for the flashlight beams dissecting it from behind her. They scan side to side and Christina studies the area. A living room with a large television hanging on the wall is all she can see. She stops when she sees movement ahead. Someone is making strange noises.

She hears scratching like on a tree or piece of wood, then a strange voice comes from the room. It sounds almost comical.

"Go away, go away, come again another day," it says.

"This is the police, and we are coming in there," she calls.

"Cops are pigs, cops are pigs," the voice calls back.

Christina shakes her head, then lowers her gun and finds a switch on the wall nearby.

When she turns on the light, she sees the largest parrot she's ever laid eyes on. It flaps its blue wings back and forth and snaps at the air, taunting them.

"Lower your weapons," she says.

The uniformed cop walks up beside her, studying the bird. It snaps its beak at him, and he pulls his finger back, narrowly missing its bite. "Damn, that thing is mean," he says.

"Don't mess with it," Christina says, "Well, this is a dead end. Let's search the place though and see if we can find out where they went. Maybe question the neighbors too, see if they've seen anything suspicious." She releases an exasperated sigh, "This is going to be a long night."

Twenty-One
The Void of Understanding

Partway into the darkness, Jessica realizes she's being followed, it's more of a feeling she can't shake. She turns to look behind her but sees nothing except waves of gray energy flowing through the air.

"Who's there?" she calls out, but no one answers. A heaviness comes over her and it's suddenly like she's walking through thick syrup.

Renay calls again and Jessica fights to move forward, finally getting free of whatever is holding her back. In a few minutes, a form appears against the darkened background. It's Renay standing there, her head moving side to side as if she's trying to find something. "Renay?" Jessica announces.

"Jessica! I couldn't find you or the house. I had to come through the bedroom mirror. How did you get in?"

"I came through my bedroom mirror, but when I wanted to leave, I couldn't find my way out. I'm stuck here and I don't know why. I've been staying at the house, playing with the children."

Renay looks at her strangely. "What do you mean playing with them? The same ones I heard in the little stones?"

"Yep, I went inside the house, and they were all there wanting to play with me. It was fun. They like to dance and play games, some old-timey ones I've never played before. I'll take you there, Renay, if you follow me."

Renay shakes her head. "No, wait, the last time I saw you was in the basement. Are you okay? You didn't show up at any of your appointments and I've been very worried. I figured they had you captive or something."

Jessica shakes her head. "They're mean, and they put me in the closet for a bit, but Wanda always does when I'm being bad. But the minute she let me out, I went straight into the mirror."

"Those bastards. They don't deserve you or any kid for that matter," Renay says. "So much has happened. Trevor, my little boy, is missing, and I think Carl had something to do with it. Did they do anything to you or bring Trevor to the house? Do you know anything or know what's going on with them?" Renay says, her words coming faster and faster. "Have you heard anything that would make you think so? Maybe have some information or something?"

Jessica looks at her wanly. "There was a man at the house right before Wanda got mean and put me in the dark closet. I think he went somewhere with Carl."

"I still can't believe they did that to you," Renay says and reaches for Jessica to put her in an embrace. Jessica would normally not like this, but things are opposite in here and it's more of a relief than it is painful.

Renay eases her grip and says to Jessica, "The police said they thought two people abducted him. Did they say where they were going?"

"I heard them through the door while I was in the closet. The door is strong, and you can't break it, but you can hear through it really well. I was so glad to get out of there. It's dark and there are spider webs everywhere. I think they said something about going over the river to Kentucky. Maybe going after Wanda and Carl's little boy, Timmy. It's weird, Renay, because Timmy is here in the house. I don't understand any of it."

Renay thinks of the information she found when looking into the Burns' and how they were found in Kentucky, dropped off by a so-called terrorist. There must be a connection.

"Well, I'm here now and I have you. We're going to get through this together, Jessica," Renay says, renewing her hug.

Jessica squeezes back, thankful for the ability to do so.

"I think the two of us can find Trevor, whether he's in Kentucky or somewhere else. We have the mirror world, and they don't. That has to be something, right? We can find them and come out of the mirror right where they are. There has to be a way."

"I'm not sure if I can, Renay. It's like my body is somewhere else. I can usually feel the tug of it when I'm ready to go, but now it's like it's everywhere or moving maybe? I can't explain it but that's what it feels like. It may explain why I've been in here so long and not tugged back into reality."

Energy ripples in waves around them, unsettling the whole area. A low growl emanates from somewhere close, and it sends shivers through Jessica, not only from the vibration it produces but a genuine fear of whatever is close by.

"What is that?" Renay asks.

"I don't know. Strange things are happening, Renay. I'm scared."

"Get close to me, Jessica, we're in this together, you and I."

The energy builds, causing Jessica and Renay to lose their balance; the floor is suddenly slanted. They stumble into each other. Jessica hugs Renay and tries to get as close as possible. The growl grows louder, and Jessica realizes it's only inches from them. Yellow eyes appear in the darkness and Jessica grabs Renay tighter, feeling the tremble of her body. The eyes raise until they are above them and looking down at Jessica and Renay.

"Jessica?" Renay says, whispering in her ear. "Do you hear that?"

Jessica is pulled along, following but wondering where they'll go. They tried before and barely escaped the creature, why did Renay think they could now? The fight or flight feeling intensifies and Jessica finds she has no choice but to go.

Jessica follows Renay for a second, then stops when she does. She thinks Renay must be as disoriented as she is and instead of running, the creature stands there for a moment and Jessica can hear its claws clicking in the darkness and can see some of its movement against the obsidian background. A slight variation of color contrasts with the shadows to make it more detectable. It's like a black panther, as the ellipses inside its eyes blink, changing size as if they are sizing them up. A cat to its prey and Jessica is overcome with a desperation to leave. Its growl is incessant and low, and Jessica hears it slash at the air in front of her; the claws coming within inches of her face. Fear grips her and she stumbles backward into Renay, holding onto her even tighter. A ripple of energy flows all around and the floor changes until they are slipping toward it instead of away. The claws cut the air again and Jessica pushes Renay to get away from them. Renay yells to her, "Run, Jessica, with me."

They slip at first but find their footing, then sprint into the dark. The growl of the creature turns into a roar. The air moves, swooshing as it leaps toward them. It lands only inches behind, and Jessica feels they won't escape this time. Renay is burning with heat and radiates pure fire from her skin, and Jessica feels as though she may not be able to hold onto the running inferno for much longer.

Jessica lets go and stumbles sideways, hearing the phantom monster growling beside her. She runs into the darkness but stops when she doesn't hear it anymore. It's going in the opposite direction away from her. The sound of clicking claws fades into the distance.

"Renay!" Jessica calls.

"I'm here," Renay says.

Jessica makes her way to where Renay is standing and feels the warmth coming from her with each hot breath she exudes.

"Are you okay?" Jessica asks.

"Yes, just warm. This place has turned up the heat," Renay says, taking large gulps of air.

Jessica takes her hand and places it on her cheek. "I think it's you. You're burning up, Renay."

"In all the craziness I never noticed, but you may be right. The scar on my stomach started getting very hot the closer the shadow creature got to me. It's really weird but I'm glad it left."

"Where do you think it went to?" Jessica asks.

Renay's breathing eases a little. "Don't know, but I hope it stays there."

Voices permeate the darkness, and Jessica recognizes them as Carl and Wanda, then another comes through. The one of the large man with the accent from the house.

"Renay, that's the man. I know him because he had a funny way of talking."

"I hear Carl and Wanda as well," Renay says. "Where's it coming from?"

"I think it's up ahead," Jessica says, pointing to the black curtain in front of them. They move slowly forward a few steps, as much as the ground will allow them to move, and see a pinprick of light.

"What is it, Jessica?" Renay asks.

"I think it's the way out. A mirror opening anyway," Jessica replies.

They take a few more arduous steps and see the opening getting larger. Suddenly a strong tug on Jessica sends both of them rolling forward head over heels. Jessica feels Renay's grip on her slipping.

"Jessica!"

Jessica can't stop herself from falling downward now.

"Jessica, watch out," Renay screams.

The creature's yellow eyes are above her and closing in fast. Jessica falls into the lit opening with the monster falling after her.

Twenty-Two
The Trade

The field lay before them, frozen with snow covering it from end to end as Carl, Wanda, and Bresnik make their way to where the stones lay. All Carl sees is a snowy field with a swollen waterway beyond. The Ohio River is nearly over its banks at the moment from recent rains and snowmelt, causing the river to become angry. Bresnik has Jessica's limp body slung over his broad shoulders like a sack of old potatoes and the mirror of souls in his other.

He leads the way like an intrepid explorer looking for a prize in the Amazon, using an outdated map. Carl watches him as he moves with caution. Bresnik says he knows where the drop-off location is, but Carl has doubts, something about the mirror has shown him.

The boy is still whimpering, and Carl can feel his shivering body every time he prods him forward.

"It'll all be over soon enough. Don't know what's over there, but it'll surely be warmer than this place.

"I'm freezing, Carl," Wanda says, "Where the hell are we anyway?"

"Shut your hole. This is the place where we lost Timmy. You don't remember because you were so messed up the last time."

"I found it," Bresnik calls out.

Carl smiles and prods the boy forward. "Come on, move your ass. Both of you."

The snow crunches beneath their feet and Carl wishes they could've brought the car out here, but the ground wouldn't allow it.

No, this one is on foot whether he likes it or not.

Carl sees Bresnik brushing away snow near the river, carefully easing to the edge of the bank but not going too far. *It'd serve the fool right if he fell in,* Carl thinks while chuckling inside. He moves on, and the cold creeps into his feet like pins sticking him. His feet are becoming numb from it though.

Tennis shoes were probably not the best choice of footwear out here and he's regretting the decision. But here they are and there's no turning back. It's not as bad as the poor kid who's in his pajamas.

When he gets to where Bresnik is still digging, it looks as though he thought to bring gloves and he's wearing boots and one of those Russian-looking hats with the flaps covering the ears. Carl wishes he had another, but instead blows on his hands in an attempt to warm them.

"You see, my friend, it was here the whole time. You remember the last time we were here? We didn't have the snow to worry about, but one can't predict the weather," Bresnik says, laughing.

Carl remembers the last time they made the trek to Salt Flat, Kentucky. This little burg was unassuming at best, but it did seem to harbor some crazy supernatural shit.

Last time he dragged Wanda out here, she was so messed up she didn't know up from down. This time, at least, she was only drinking. It made her mean but not as loopy.

The thing that came from the air he couldn't explain. It was pure darkness, and he doubted he could've seen it all if not for its yellow eyes protruding through the shadowy backdrop. It stood at least ten feet tall but that was an exaggeration as it had no real form. The creature didn't possess a skeleton, but it moved as gracefully as a cloud on a rainy day, only faster. To this day, Carl couldn't explain if asked. It was a thing but nothing more, almost a ghost if he had any other words for it. He wasn't sure he wanted to see it again. "Come on, help me dig," Bresnik says, then reaches into his pockets. He produces another set of gloves and throws them to Carl.

"Fuck that," Carl says and turns to Wanda, handing her the gloves. "Start digging woman."

"Me?" Wanda says, holding the gloves in front of her.

"Yes, you. I have to hold the kid and keep him from running off."

Wanda slowly puts the gloves on and kneels beside Bresnik. The Albanian looks back at Carl with disgust but continues to dig along with Wanda. Carl doesn't care.

The boy squirms, trying to free himself from Carl's grip but he doubles down and holds him tighter. "Stop moving you little shit, this'll be over soon enough."

Carl watches as the stones in front of the grouping are uncovered. The one in front is the most prominent as words are inscribed on it. Carl remembers this from the last time he was here. Bresnik read from it and said some other things. It was a different language—German if he remembered correctly. Not long after, Timmy disappeared into the night.

"Now we're getting somewhere," Bresnik says. He stands and turns toward Carl. "All I got to do is say the words and aim the mirror in the right direction. Bring the girl over."

Carl leaves the boy with Wanda and grabs Jessica's limp body, bringing it close to where Bresnik stands and looks at the small stone that resembles a grave marker. He can't read what it says but knows Bresnik can, so he shrugs instead.

"Well, get to it then, before we all freeze to death."

Bresnik laughs. "In my country, this is early fall. You Americans are too spoiled," he says, waving a dismissive hand. Bresnik reaches into his pocket and pulls out a flashlight. He turns it on and shines it at the stone. It lights up, nearly glowing as he studies the thing intently, then sets the mirror beside the grave marker.

"Bresnik?" Carls says, "What makes you think that monster won't do like it did the last time? I'm not feeling too good about this."

"Because I have the Mirror of Souls. This will work as a homing beacon for the girl and the changeling will follow like a hungry animal, trying to capture the girl's soul. Once we have it trapped, we can bargain with it better and get your son back. I didn't have it last time. I assure you, this time will be different."

Carl shakes his head, "So, why did we bring the boy?"

"For the trade. It will want the girl's soul but will have to chase it in the other realm. The boy is an instant trade for your son. Trust me, friend, I know what I'm doing."

Carl is not relieved by this statement, knowing the past debacles Bresnik has led them through. He hates to admit it, but Wanda may be right about him.

Bresnik angles the mirror upward and says, "Come, oh ancient one to the Mirror of Souls!" He stands back.

A hum invades Carl's ears, irritating but tolerable as the night begins to ripple, and shadowy waves roll like a brackish ocean in the air in front of them. Carl stumbles backward as a huge claw breaks the night.

It's dark like a shadow but intact enough to take his head off or at least it seems. He's not taking chances.

Wanda screams at the sudden appearance of the monster, then begins shaking and crying.

"What is that thing?" she says.

"Bresnik? Do something! Keep that thing away from us."

Bresnik grabs hold of Jessica and pushes her forward toward the mirror. The changeling stops in midair and hovers, staring at them with monstrous yellow eyes as the mirror emits a light around it and the gravestone glows with it, combining in a soup of brilliance.

"Yes, I have your attention now, don't I?" Bresnik says.

Jessica's eyes flutter open, and she breathes in a sudden gasp like she's waking from a long dream. Carl watches Bresnik, smiling like he's won a great prize.

"The girl and the mirror keep it at bay," he says to Carl, then turns to the shadow creature. "We have something for you. A sort of trade, if you will. One of your children for this one."

He motions and Carl sees his cue. He pushes the boy forward so the monster can see him. Trevor cries uncontrollably, protesting under his gag.

The creature looks at him and then at Bresnik. Strangled words form as it tries to speak. "Remember you I do. Got away last time," the thing says, then looks at Trevor. "Children, this for this?" it says like it's speaking in a riddle. "Boy for Boy?"

"What the hell is it talking about Bresnik?" Carl says, "Do something."

"Shut up, you idiot, it wants to do the trade. Can you not understand what it's saying?"

"Hey, you don't talk to me that way," Carl says but stops when he notices the creature looming over him. His resolve weakens and he trembles as the thing reaches with its black claw and grasps the boy from him. He falls forward, not expecting the sudden pull, and Carl's knees sink into the cold wet snow.

He crawls backward, trying to regain his footing.

The creature holds Trevor whose gag has fallen out of his mouth. His wrists and ankles are still bound, and he struggles with all the strength he can muster, screaming to the top of his lungs, mixing with Wanda's nonstop crying.

Carl feels sorry for the boy and can only imagine what the monster will do to him.

While holding the boy, the thing considers Carl and Bresnik, even the screaming Wanda behind them.

"The girl? Is she the trade?" it says to Bresnik.

He turns to Jessica. "Yes, the girl too, if it makes you happy," he says then under his breath, "Go find her you piece of shit."

The phantom opens its black mouth, showing nothing but light from the stones and the mirror pulsing a glow around it ... Its substance no more than that of a shadow.

Sharp talons on the end of its hand extend toward Bresnik like it's going to strike him, but it hesitates like it can't go beyond the light. The creature looks at him and then gingerly pulls Jessica's body toward it.

Bresnik winces but relinquishes his hold on her.

She does little to protest against it, and to Carl, she looks like she can't, like all the fire is taken from her. The creature eases the children into the darkness of its body then turns toward Bresnik. It raises its dark hand, but before it can bring it down on him, he takes a rock he's hiding behind him and smashes the mirror. The light goes out and the changeling disappears into the air.

Screeching sounds echo through the night and the area is plunged into darkness again with only the dim moon showing through the winter clouds.

"So, is that it, Bresnik? Where is our kid, where is Timmy?" Carl asks.

The Albanian looks at the air in front of him where the energy remnants the monster came from are still rippling and the mirror is glowing.

"I'm not sure. I thought it would stay around longer." The gravestones begin glowing and Bresnik turns to Carl, "See, your Timmy will be coming next," he says then stops. The big man quivers and tries to speak. "I ... I don't ..." he says, then screams in agony.

Carl's eyes widen as he sees the black hand come through Bresnik's middle. His body sizzles and pops like bubbling acid while the monster's dark appendage moves in a circular motion, working its way around the guts and bodily fluids it contacts.

Blood splashes onto Carl's face, causing him to gag, as the creature's hand appears from the middle of Bresnik's abdomen.

Blood and water gush over the front of the shaking man, falling against the snow below and mixing outward like some weird abstract painting.

Wanda wails fresh screams that echo through the night as the creature pulls its arm out of Bresnik and the man first falls to his knees, then flops limply face down in the snow with a thud.

Carl stares unbelievingly at the large hole in Bresnik's back, then back at the creature.

"Tempt me not. Boy is yours, be home tonight." The thing says, then dissolves into the night back through the fabric from which it came.

Twenty-Three
Renay in peril

Jessica feels herself being pulled in different directions all at once while being taken back into the upside-down world. The dark tendrils of the creature enter her mind and take over, turning her into a puppet. It's controlling everything, her body, emotions, and she has no way of freeing herself. She wishes now she had never come here, as what seems like an escape is becoming a prison.

The shadow monster is like an animal working on pure instinct. It's more than her mind can fathom and it's scary to her.

The monster doesn't have her completely yet, but it will soon, and Jessica knows somewhere deep inside she only has a short time before the thing consumes her.

Jessica pulls away from the phantom, feeling its grip loosening, and falls away into the darkness, landing in the field close to the house.

"Jessica? Are you alright? Where did you go?"

Jessica rolls to her side and sits upright. Renay is standing there, extending a hand in assistance. "I fell from the mirror into my physical body, but I'm back and the two aren't separate anymore. It feels funny but normal at the same time. I wonder if when I go back, I'll be normal like everyone else."

"What do you mean, with no Autism?" Renay asks.

"Yes, that's it exactly. I love the things I can do here and the fact I'm not burdened by anything holding me back. Wouldn't it be wonderful, Renay? If I go back and I'm like any other girl?"

Renay stares at her, "But, Jessica, that's what makes you unique. If not for your ability to see the world in the way you do, we wouldn't be together, and I would never find Trevor. I like you just the way you are.

We're both broken and need each other to stand tall. I love you, Jessica, in every way, you're the mirror to my soul."

Jessica smiles and takes Renay's hand, and she helps her to her feet. "I love you too, Renay, for helping me and not judging me like so many do."

"C'mon, girl, let's get my little boy."

Jessica nods and turns her attention to the house sitting in the distance in the same position as before, upside down and floating.

The horizon is moving like clouds before a thunderstorm, all gray on a stark black background. It all meets in an unsettling mess over the house.

Renay turns to Jessica. "What's going on? Why is everything moving like that?"

"I don't know. Things have taken a strange turn," she replies.

"Come on, let's go to the house and see if we can find Trevor," Renay says.

Jessica walks with her but before they get to their destination, a shadow blackens the sky above them. Renay stops and motions for Jessica to be quiet. The phantom hovers over the house for a moment, holding Trevor, then disappears into the structure.

"Trevor!" Renay calls out, "We really need to go in there now," Renay says, then grips her stomach and cries out in agony.

Jessica's face throbs and she places a hand over it. "What's wrong? I'm scared. I have a strange feeling about all of this."

Renay crouches beside Jessica and takes a deep breath. "Listen, I have you. Don't worry," she says. Tears fill her eyes. "We need to hold on for each other's sake. It's the only way we'll get through this." Renay pulls Jessica in close for a tight embrace. She releases her and stands. "Now, come on, we have to get in that house."

Jessica wonders if now that her physical body is in here as well, will she wake up if something happens or will she be stuck here forever? The thought isn't very comforting.

The gravestones come to life, singing with a chorus from the children, *"Come to us and join the fun,"* they say in a singsong chorus.

The joy and happiness have changed to dread, masking their true intention.

Jessica squeezes Renay, staying as close as possible. The turmoil inside her, causes something dark to tug on her, but she keeps it to herself.

They step onto the porch and the house, as always, rights itself. Light energy crackles underneath the old boards and Jessica feels Renay's hesitation and her body heating up, but they press on and open the front door.

Giggling voices clamor on the other side of the room beyond the hallway where the dining room sits.

"Do you hear that, Jessica?" Renay says.

Jessica nods. "It's my friends. They laugh a lot, but in a weird way, like they want to play tricks all the time. They tell me they do on adults but not kids."

"Well, that's refreshing," Renay says.

Jessica's nerves are on edge and the sound of the children does little to settle them. She not only hears but feels their true intent and it's unsettling. But somewhere deep inside her, it feels normal, the same as breathing, and this disturbs her even more.

They move cautiously toward the door when it opens and a dim light floods the room, showing the floor. The brightness reveals small bugs scuttling away into the darkest corners of the room. In the doorway, a small boy stands, his figure casting a stretched shadow.

"Timmy?" Jessica says.

"You know him?" Renay asks.

"Yes, he's Carl and Wanda's son. I think he's ready to go home."

"Home?" Renay asks. "How long has he been here?"

"I don't know, but I have a feeling it's been long enough for him to not be the son they once knew," Jessica says.

The boy doesn't acknowledge them, only steps toward the open front door. His walk turns to a run, and he sprints through, leaping from the porch onto the open field beyond. He disappears into the darkness.

"That was strange even by this place's standards," Renay says. "Come on, Jessica, let's go. We have to find Trevor."

Jessica follows Renay, unsure of what to do and ignoring the gnawing of dark thoughts entering her mind. There are rubbery tendrils filling her like some foreign entity with desires she doesn't understand.

Almost a bloodlust of sorts. They walk into the hallway that's dingy with corners full of cobwebs and dust. A set of stairs is at the end, descending into who knows where. Two doors are on either side of the hall.

Trevor's voice echoes from somewhere ahead. "Mommy! Come get me!"

"Mommy's coming baby, hang on," Renay calls out.

They go toward the stairs, walking past the doors open to the rooms inside. Jessica peeks into one, the mirror room, and sees it being empty. In the other, the children are sitting on one side of the table like they are ready to eat dinner. The nanny stands on the other side of the children, ready to round them up if need be.

They regard her for a second before returning to stare at empty plates and nonexistent food. They have deep dark eyes void of any other color like obsidian pools of never-ending darkness. Jessica feels their dark hearts beating and their longing for sustenance and it makes her tremble inside, but another feeling is there as well. The need to get it for them.

It sounds like Trevor is calling from below somewhere. Renay walks toward the stairway and Jessica stays close behind, nearly attached to her back.

When they reach the bottom, an area eerily like the basement Jessica is forced to stay in, lays out before them. There is even an old, dingy mattress in the middle with stains all over it. Trevor calls from the other side of the basement, from a mirror leaning against the wall. His hands are against the glass inside and he looks like he is trying to reach out.

"I'm coming, Trevor!" Renay starts to run for the other side.

Jessica runs after her. "Wait, Renay, I think it's a trick."

Renay jumps toward the mirror. As her hands touch it, though, she can't seem to stop and tumbles headfirst into a film of shining light.

Jessica stands there panting, wondering what will come next.

Twenty-Four
Timmy's Home

The dark veil is still rippling from where the creature vanished through it. Lying in the field below the shadowy area is the cold lifeless body of Bresnik lying next to the mirror, the light gone from it, as void of life as the big man bleeding in the snow.

Carl grabs Wanda by the arm. "I think it's time to go," he says, before hoisting her to her feet.

"But what about, Timmy? Isn't that what we came for?" she says.

"Yep, but I think we've been duped," Carl says, then turns toward the car. Wanda stands there for a moment and Carl shakes his head. "Come on. This won't get us anywhere. Maybe we'll come back tomorrow when the weather changes." He takes a step toward the vehicle a good five hundred feet away and stops when he hears Wanda cry out.

"Timmy! My boy, come to Momma!"

Carl turns to see a boy standing there in the dark. Wanda has her phone out and the flashlight on, but Carl only sees a partially lit figure standing there. His silhouette contrasts against the horizon, making his body more shadow than substance. He watches as Wanda reaches for the boy.

"Hey, Wanda, wait a second."

It's already too late. Wanda grabs Timmy, ready to envelop him in an embrace, but before she can, she screams and drops the phone.

The crack resounds throughout the open space, undeniably the sound of a bone splintering.

In the partial light of the phone, blood spews in a large gush from the side of Wanda's neck as she tries to squirm away.

The boy pushes her to the ground with strength he should not possess, then jumps on top of her. His hands are like claws.

Talons that remind Carl of their parrot at home. Shivers of panic run through him as his son snarls and growls while tearing at the flesh of his wife.

"Carl! Help me!" she gurgles, but Carl can't move. He is frozen stiff with fear. Her protests turn to garbled speech, as Timmy rips out her throat and gnaws on the bloody flesh. He spits and looks at Carl. A black grinning mouth with blood dripping from it is all he sees, illuminated in the partially lit area.

He's seen enough and reaches for his pistol but finds it's not there, having opted to leave it in the car. Carl turns and runs for the vehicle with every bit of fear-induced power he has in him. He makes it halfway there before slipping in the snow and falling, sliding forward with arms splayed above his head.

He scrambles on his hands and knees, then screams as Timmy's teeth sink deep into the flesh of his calve muscle. He swings a fist at him, connecting with the side of his head.

Timmy yelps and falls from him, rolling to the side. Carl takes advantage of the distraction and jumps to his feet. Pain pulses from his leg, but he tries to ignore it, focusing only on the gun in the car.

Snarling like some rabid animal invades his ears, sending fresh tremors through his body. He hobbles the rest of the way to the car, opens the passenger side door, and lunges inside, reaching for the center console.

Timmy is on him and bites the other leg, sending a fresh torrent of sharp pain through his body. Carl points the gun toward Timmy and aims, careful not to blow off the leg his son is working on. The gun fires inside the car, hitting Timmy square between the eyes.

Carl screams through ringing ears, gritting his teeth as pain throbs, sharp and unrelenting through his lower leg. He stares unbelievingly at the missing toes the gun took off and yells as loud as he can, "Timmy!"

He should never have trusted, Bresnik, but knows it's too late to second guess himself. Carl sits up, groaning at his throbbing legs, the cold biting at them and providing a fresh torrent of pain. They look as though they've been obliterated by explosives, and he knows he'll need a hospital as soon as possible.

To prevent shooting himself again, he puts the gun on the dashboard and pulls his body into the car with his arms until he's behind the wheel, then reaches into his pocket to get the keys, wincing at the amount of pain his body is experiencing.

He clicks the key forward and stops, hearing something growl behind him. Carl turns his head to the side to see a mouth full of sharp black teeth widen. He screams as they sink into his face.

Twenty-Five
Awakenings

Renay finds herself in a room, staring unbelievingly into the eyes of her dead ex-husband. This has to be a trick. It can't be real. One of his eyes is missing. All that remains is a blackened hole. The other is glassy with a cataract glaze covering it.

"Renay, quit fighting, Trevor is right where he needs to be ... with his father," Mike says.

Renay looks around the room. It's Trevor's old bedroom. Everything looks the same way she remembers it being, even the aquarium under the window. In the entrance door of the room, she sees something she can't comprehend. A little girl about the age of two toddles in front of her.

Oh God, Molly Renay.

The toddler wobbles to her and Renay reaches down but is struck with a sharp pain in her midsection. She raises her shirt and sees the scar where the monster's claws contacted her is glowing red. Renay hugs her stomach and rocks in agony.

"It's just like you always wanted. A baby girl to hold. A sister for Trevor. Molly Renay will live here with him forever. They won't grow old or worry about anything ever again," Mike says.

Renay fights to see through the pain and tears. To maybe get some kind of explanation for what is happening to her. This can't be right, it's all wrong.

"No, Mike," she screams, partly in protest and also from the intense pain she feels. "You don't get to make that call. You had your chance, and I don't have to listen to you. Trevor, come to Mommy!"

Trevor appears for a second, then disappears again. The room suddenly spins in a vortex and Renay feels herself descending. Her legs are wobbly and unstable as she goes down through a small drainpipe, or at least that's what it looks like. The tug is strong and incessant, and she cannot resist it.

A crushing feeling takes over and she feels the air leaving her lungs. She takes one last gulp before losing sight of the room. A flash of light and she drops, falling onto her butt in the dining room. But it was above her before, right? Renay can't make sense of where she is, right side or upside down. This place defies explanation.

⚬

Jessica has lost her way after she watched Renay disappear into the mirror against the wall and now, she's alone with only her thoughts. Jessica looks around the room for anything important but finds it empty. The walls are bare, with only dirt and rocks, ancient-looking with no plaster as you'd find in a regular home.

Boxes are stacked in the corner with mildew and decay creeping up the edge, blackening the brown cardboard, like the decay she feels inside. A despair she can't understand. Her entire life she has had no way to regulate her emotions, only ways to cause herself pain to make it all go away.

Now, she feels what it's like to hold onto the feelings inside her and Jessica doesn't care for it.

Jessica goes to the mirror and places a hand against the glass, but nothing happens and this time the mirror doesn't pull her in.

She calls to Renay but gets no answer, then stands and hears someone behind her.

Jessica turns to see a woman standing there. Her hair is disheveled, and she looks emaciated with bruises on her arms and legs.

She smiles and shows a mouthful of blackened teeth and seems to be out of time like she is only a ghost of a former life. Her stomach is distended and pregnant. She looks as though she should be delivering soon.

The woman is familiar to Jessica as if she is looking at an older reflection of herself. Is this her real mother? Jessica's intrigue piques when she notices the woman is no longer pregnant but holding her baby and talking to it.

The scene switches to her mother standing by a car with a man in it. The car is new, and the man looks well put together like someone of importance. He's motioning for her mother to go inside a building.

"There, there, girl. All will be good. You need to understand, Jessica, this isn't over. We'll be back together soon, I promise. The good folks at the adoption agency will take care of you and raise you like their own until a family adopts you. Then, I'll talk to a lawyer about getting you back. I have a few jobs to do and can't take you with me, but I promise we'll be a family soon."

The car with the man in it honks and her mother disappears inside with Jessica in her arms. Was this what Wanda was talking about? Had Jessica's mother been abducted, taken away by the man or did she willingly give Jessica away, knowing she would never come back to claim her?

The questions weigh on Jessica like bricks.

Tears form in Jessica's eyes, and she wants so badly to reach out and touch the woman and then hold her. This is something she's never felt before. The upside-down world is affecting her in ways she doesn't know how to overcome. The feelings are overwhelming for her, and she tries to focus, keep it all together, but the emotion is too much, and she begins to cry.

"Momma," she wails. "Momma don't go away and leave me. I need you!" Jessica falls to her knees and sobs uncontrollably, not understanding where it all comes from.

Somewhere deep inside where the emotion is trapped. A place she keeps away from the outside world because she has no choice. The body she inhabits won't allow it, but in here, things are backward, upside down, so all is the opposite of what Jessica is used to.

The woman pays no attention to her, only disappears into the wall away from Jessica, and the newfound loss in her heart she feels.

Jessica sniffs and tries to dry her tears but her breath hitches, making it hard to stop the stream of hurt. She stands and walks to the wall, then touches it, massaging her fingers across the rough surface of mud and clay.

Jessica hangs her head feeling a longing deep inside for something she's never known. The scar on her face is burning like an unquenchable fire.

Her mother was always an enigma to her and only an afterthought until this encounter. The hurt she feels and the sense of loss for someone who was lost with nowhere to turn, will stay with her for a while.

Why did the house have to show this to her? Jessica would've been fine without it.

Maybe something broke free a memory lodged deep in her brain somewhere or maybe she'd been harboring the baggage all her life and now is able to release it. Either way, it's a burden she doesn't want or need anymore.

There's a thump on the floor above her and Jessica turns for the stairs, runs up, hoping Renay has returned.

Twenty-Six
Seven Years of Bad Luck

Jessica runs to the room and sees Renay sitting on the floor, dazed but otherwise fine. "Renay, this place is going insane. It's angry, not welcoming like before. I want to go."

Renay shakes her head. "Not without Trevor, Jessica. He's here somewhere and I have to find him."

"But what if you can't? I'm worried the phantom might be planning on keeping Trevor the same way as he did Timmy.

Several of the children told me they had been here for years, and they don't even know what year it is outside of this world."

"No. I won't think that way. We have to get Trevor back no matter what kind of craziness this thing throws at us."

"I'm sorry, but I don't want to be here anymore. I'm scared, Renay. I've never been afraid before or even knew how to feel it, but now, it's all I can think about."

Renay crouches in front of Jessica. "Listen, it's going to be okay. We've come too far to back out now. We have to get Trevor. It's the only way," Renay says. "Now, come on, let's check out the next room and see if there is another way to find him."

Jessica nods and follows Renay out of the room and into the hallway. They cross the hall and enter the next room where Jessica remembers playing with the kids the last time she was there. This time instead of one large mirror in the middle, there are several set up on the walls like outside the house.

They all reflect Renay and Jessica's image back at them. The large one though has something else in it. The house is there but instead of being upside down, it's right side up and there is movement around it. It's like a movie playing in black and white, flashing in and out like an old silent picture. They look at each other, the thought of two souls forever connected in this event, then step toward the mirror. Jessica feels the familiar tug she always does when going into the mirror and is swallowed up by it with Renay following after.

Twenty-Seven
Diving into the Past

Renay stands after being tossed to the ground from tumbling out of the mirror. Jessica is beside her, on her feet and Renay reaches for her hand, squeezing it tight. The old house looms in front of them with a child running through the yard.

The house looks newer like it hasn't seen the battering of too much age and it prompts Renay to think this is the past when it was new.

Two adults sit on the porch, a man and a woman. The man puffs on a pipe, drawing it in as he lights the top with a match. Smoke releases from the side of his clenched mouth and rolls around his head, dissipating into the air.

The woman is smiling, watching the child play and they seem very content. The way a family should be. Crops of corn and other vegetables grow nearby in neat rows, the green leafy stalks, blowing gently in the wind. The scene is peaceful and serene.

Renay spots a shed close by with a German name on it, Glashuette, it says. The same as she saw in the newspaper article. It translates to Glassworks. It's the man who made mirrors.

The sky gets darker and clouds form around the house. They move quickly, blurring the late summer day, and blotting out the sun.

When the sky settles again, a horrific picture plays out in front of Renay's vision.

In the distance, the woman hangs there with a child next to her with two nooses tight around their necks and their heads in a tilted position.

The clouds roll again, and the air is electric with static, crackling like it's on fire. The woman and the girl blur and disappear and the air begins to calm down.

The next scene is the man hammering nails into the side of the house, then hanging the mirrors, eventually working around the house until every inch is covered. The woman is nowhere to be seen, and the child is gone too.

The house is bleak and the sky around it is devoid of the joy it once had. The man sits on the porch, staring into space, seeming to be lost in some universe of despair, then he appears in the tree where the woman and child hung, a noose around his neck as well.

The tree rots and falls, branch by branch to the dry dirt below. The field around it is overgrown and devoid of crops, only weedy vegetation remains.

The clouds around the house get heavier until the structure is nearly covered. Then a large, black-clawed hand comes over the top of the place and pulls upward, releasing the house from its moorings. The whole scene turns upside down, house and all until the ground is above the house and the roof is upside-down.

Both Renay and Jessica hold the scarred areas of their bodies as a sudden jolt of pain invades and they are sucked into the house.

The shadow monster laughs, and they can't stop the descent toward it. "Fight it, Jessica," Renay says and reaches for anything she can find to gain purchase. She grabs the door facing the entrance of the house with one hand and Jessica with the other. "Hold on! Don't let go!"

Renay inches toward the outside, pulling with every ounce of energy she has, ignoring the blinding pain of her midsection and the strain this is putting on her arms.

From somewhere deep inside she finds unknown strength and manages to get her and Jessica to the front porch. The pull of the house lessens, and she nudges Jessica toward the front yard.

Once there, they turn to look at the house as it heaves like it's breathing. Children run from the house, turning into large black bugs crawling from the cracks of the place and running over the sides of the house and along the ground in different directions.

Renay grips Jessica's hand tighter, "C'mon, let's go!"

The bugs are falling into a hole of some sort just beyond the yard. Renay runs toward the opening, pulling Jessica with her.

They jump into the hole and roll out onto the floor of the house, jumping to their feet while the black invaders fall around them.

The insects spill out over the frame and toward Renay and Jessica's feet. They jump away, as the creatures touch their shoes.

Renay kicks at one and sends it spiraling into the wall where it hits with a crack and rolls onto the ground. It runs away trying to find some place to hide in the dark corner.

Renay loses her grip on Jessica's hand, realizing she's pulled away and is retrieving something —a loose brick. Darkness covers the mirror behind the bugs, pouring out into the room.

Renay turns to Jessica who is lifting a hand with the brick in it. Jessica lets loose and throws the projectile into the mirror. Glass shatters and smashes in shards onto the floor, and somewhere in the house they hear a scream. The walls shudder and then go still as the dark retreats in that mirror and begins to come from the others.

Renay nods to Jessica to pick up the brick again and smiles as she smashes another.

Shrill screams shake the house and the boards shudder underneath their feet. This time though, Renay frowns as Jessica winces in pain and Renay's scar heats up with new fire.

Twenty-Eight
Breaking Out

Jessica drops her hand with the brick in it to her side and shakes off the hurt. She gets it now. The mirrors keep the house alive and the creature going! It makes perfect sense, and she kicks herself for not seeing it before. The children are trapped inside them and somehow their trauma and hers is reflected upon this place.

It all makes sense, the reason she felt pain when smashing the mirror is because she's inextricably connected to the creature and the house itself.

The revelation is part understanding and partly the fact she's given the information because of her connection, she realizes, to the shadow creature. She wants no part of it, wants only to be separated from the thing.

It's time to break free!

Jessica raises her hand again and takes aim at the next mirror.

"Jessica, what are you doing?" Renay asks.

"Striking back. The house and the creature need the mirrors to stay alive."

"I see what you mean, but won't it hurt you too?"

Jessica shrugs, "I don't care, the only way to get your son back is to break the hold the phantom has on him. The mirrors on and in the house are what gives it power, so we have to destroy them!"

Jessica lets the brick fly, and it flips end over end, landing in the middle of another mirror, shattering the glass in a brilliant display of fine shards.

Something strange begins to occur, and the remaining mirrors vanish one by one, fading upward like sand falling upside down in an hourglass.

The bugs keep coming from cracks and crevices and covering the floor until they are ankle-deep. Jessica manages to get the brick before it vanishes in the mix of the black wave.

Renay and Jessica step around them, heading for the door and running across the threshold and into the hallway toward the main room of the house. The bugs are still coming, clicking against each other and producing loud chittering sounds. When they get to the door of the room, they walk through and slam it behind them.

"I think the house, or the creature is fighting to keep us. Renay, I only know this because my mind is still my own. I don't know how much longer that will be."

"What do you mean? Is that thing controlling you?"

"No, not yet, but I feel a connection to it, one I can't explain. It's like it's drawing me to it," Jessica says. "Renay? I don't think it will let go of Trevor, at least not easily. I feel the urges it has inside of me and there will be no stopping. It has us both in here now and we won't wake up. It isn't a dream anymore. I think it wants to suck us dry of any life we ever had."

Renay starts to speak but is cut off by the sound of Trevor calling to her. "Come on, it sounds like he's upstairs," Renay says reaching for the door. The one where the bugs were only moments ago.

"Renay, don't open that door!" Jessica says, but it's too late. The door creaks wide to reveal a hallway again. No bugs in sight, only old boards leading up to a stairway, but instead of going down, it goes up.

"There. He's upstairs this time," Renay says as if this is normal.

Jessica shakes her head, realizing it's another trick. The creature is playing with them, like mice in a maze. Jessica notices a piece of mirror lying on the ground, scattering from the mirror room where they had been earlier. She reaches for it and retrieves it, tucking it in her pocket the best she can. Now, she has the brick and a piece of the mirror to use, and knowing what she did earlier had hurt the house and the creature, both should come in handy. Jessica runs to catch up to Renay.

Renay stops at the stairs and Jessica steps beside her. They go halfway up to a landing and then change direction and continue to the top. Trevor calls again and Renay turns to Jessica. "This will all be over soon, I promise."

Jessica nods and they begin to ascend the steps together. She hopes Renay is right, but she has no illusion it may not turn out the way they want. Either way, Jessica and Renay are in this together no matter the outcome.

Twenty-Nine
Jessica fights Back

The room at the top of the stairs is more like an attic, small with sloping ceilings that extend to the sides. Mirrors adorn every side of the room except one. Trevor is there, held by the shadow creature, as he struggles to free himself, his eyes wide and tears soaking his cheeks.

Renay runs for him, but the creature won't allow it and shoves her back, causing her to fall on her bottom, arms to her sides. Jessica steps forward next, but slower, more deliberate, walking to the middle of the room and speaking to the creature, "Can you please let him go?"

The creature studies her, appearing to consider what Jessica is saying. "Done, trade is. Mine, this child," it replies in a disjointed language as it struggles to form words.

Jessica feels fear pulsing through the monster like it's a caged animal. An overwhelming feeling of dread permeates from it and Jessica has some sympathy for the thing.

"He's not yours," Renay cries out.

Jessica hugs Renay. "It doesn't understand what you are saying. It's like a wild animal, backed into a corner and ready to strike. I have to go to it, maybe it will release Trevor if it gets me instead."

Renay considers her and shakes her head. "No, that's not an option, we leave here together."

"Okay, but if it lets him go, grab Trevor and don't look back. I have a plan," Jessica says and shows Renay the brick.

Jessica points to the mirrors and she sees understanding dawn on Renay's face. "Do what you have to," Renay says.

Jessica steps toward the creature, calmly, even though inside her mind is filled with things she can't understand. Thoughts and emotions fill her with terror, something she's never been able to comprehend. All Jessica has ever known is to lash out and hurt herself when this happened. Her stomach is fluttering like the sensation of a hundred butterflies inside of her.

A quick thought comes to mind, will she be able to explore this feeling or will this end today? Something she would never have thought of before. Jessica takes a deep breath and gets ready to say her piece. "I offer another trade. Me for him and we will leave this place," Jessica says.

The shadowy figure floats in front of her, its mass as large as the room itself, like the nighttime stretches to the horizon on a winter's day. Nothing is seen beyond it, only a vastness no human can comprehend.

"This, you, boy trade?" The creature says.

"Yes, me for him and we'll leave."

Its yellow eyes dart back and forth around the room then it settles back on Jessica.

"Mine, this one, two you, her too," it says, pointing at Renay.

Jessica shakes her head, turns, raises the brick, and lets the projectile go. It flies through the air and hits the closest mirror, shattering the glass into pieces, causing the creature to scream like it's been cut deeply.

Jessica runs to retrieve the brick and turns back to the creature. She raises the brick again, aiming for another mirror.

"I'll smash them all if you don't let the boy go!"

The creature is visibly upset at the turn of events. Jessica feels this as well as sees it based on the gnawing inside of her gut, causing pain to radiate through her body and her cheek to flare.

The phantom hesitates, though, and Jessica throws the brick into another mirror.

The creature howls when it smashes, and she grabs the brick again and raises it toward the last mirror in the room.

"Wait! Acceptable, this," it says and eases Trevor toward Jessica.

The gamble is paying off and Jessica walks toward the creature, passing Trevor, as he rolls away from the shadows' long reach.

Jessica smiles when she sees Renay grab her son, both crying uncontrollably in an embrace that makes Jessica feel wonderful inside. The creature wastes no time and pulls Jessica into its embrace and energy is siphoned from her immediately. If she doesn't strike now, she'll be too weak in a few seconds.

"Run, Renay!"

Jessica throws the brick one last time. A loud shriek echoes through the air around them when the projectile makes contact with the glass. Pieces of the mirror explode in a brilliant spray and the creature recoils.

She seizes the opportunity to jump away from the phantom but stumbles as the house violently shakes. Renay is at the top step of the stairs with Trevor in her arms and Jessica runs toward her but is suddenly stopped. She looks down to find a black tendril wrapped around her ankle, gripping her tightly enough that she knows she won't be able to get away. "Run," she calls out to Renay.

The house screams painfully and reverberates with fresh tremors as Jessica is pulled toward the shadow monster. She reaches for something to grab but there is nothing. The house is falling apart, but the creature is still very much there and real.

Jessica grabs the only weapon she has; the broken piece of mirror tucked in her pocket.

She jabs it into the black tentacle holding her ankle and the creature eases its grip for a second, but two more strands lash out and grab her arms. Another flies past her and wraps around Renay.

The rope around one of her hands eases when the creature grabs Renay and Jessica is able to pull the hand with the piece of glass in it away. She wastes no time and cuts the strand holding Renay.

The phantom screams in agony, letting go of Renay but doubling its efforts on Jessica instead. It wraps another around her throat and forces her into an awkward position with both hands and her head held.

She cranes her neck toward the stairway and is relieved to see Renay and Trevor are gone. Jessica has enough finger movement to manipulate the glass to cut the tendril holding her wrist.

When the creature releases her this time, she slashes at it and brings fresh screams with each strike. This pains her as well, but she doesn't stop. Jessica endures self-abuse all the time, this is nothing for her and she cuts at it again and again, watching as it retreats. The creature's resolve weakens, and she believes the shadow is finally letting go.

Jessica takes advantage of this and leaps for the stairway that bucks and cracks, sending splinters of wood into the air.

The floor heaves but she doesn't let it stop her. Jessica is almost to the stairs when she feels the overwhelming weight of the creature surround her. It wraps around her legs and pulls her backward. She brings the piece of glass in front of her ready to strike.

This one is for Renay, Trevor, and all of the children this abomination has held in its grimy grasp. The power it has to siphon the life from them ends today when Jessica deals it one last blow.

THIRTY
RENAY ESCAPES

Renay stumbles down the steps taking them two at a time with Trevor close behind, gripping his hand so tight she fears she'll cut off the blood flow.

She doesn't care though, all that matters is getting out of this house. They are at the front door and on the porch before she realizes Jessica isn't with them.

Renay pulls Trevor close to her, knowing if she goes back, then the whole gesture is for nothing.

Jessica is going up against something neither of them understands. She picks Trevor up, cradling him in her arms, and steps off the porch, then hesitates and looks back at the house.

It's upside down again but instead of hovering steadily where it usually does, it's much shakier. The mirrors are all busted, and pieces of glass lie broken everywhere and the house moves erratically before it begins to crush inward upon itself.

The sky around it cracks like a windshield spider webbing outward into the unknown.

The ground is cracking below their feet as well, and Renay fears the whole place is coming apart.

She renews her grip on Trevor and runs toward the field as the gravestones beside the house moan their discontent with the situation as if they understand the impending doom.

Renay grips her son tighter, running as far away from the house and this place as possible. Ripples of energy crackle in the charged air like static on a sweater, but Renay keeps going. The black field seems to swallow them whole and the tall, dark grass delights in this as it thrashes wildly around them.

The world tilts and moves back and forth across the expanse of black.

Ahead, a barely perceptible gray spot mars the otherwise solid black background. Renay focuses on it, hoping salvation lies beyond.

She holds Trevor tighter than she ever has even as she stumbles forward on wobbly legs.

Pieces of black glass fly through the air, hitting Renay and sending dark shards into her face. One lodges in her cheek, and she cries out, but keeps going.

Once she gets to the off-color spot, Renay extends her hand toward it and is pleased when the spot gives a little and she realizes it's definitely the portal she's looking for.

"We're going through, baby," she says to Trevor, "Are you ready? "Trevor cries, holding her around the neck tightly. "Okay, Mommy."

Renay turns to take another glance at the upside-down world and watches as the whole place continues to roll in on itself. The house is gone and so is Jessica. A realization she has a hard time accepting. Tears moisten her eyes as Renay jumps headfirst into the gray beyond.

She falls forward, tumbling onto solid ground and losing her grip on Trevor. Renay jumps to her feet and frantically searches for him and is relieved to see him crouching on the ground close by.

The sky is gray but lighter than in the world where they had come from. It's near dawn and she's sure the sky will light up soon when the sun rises behind the gray winter backdrop.

The sound of water flows nearby and Renay can see the shape of a meandering river in the shadows of the pre-dawn day. Snow flurries fly around her head as Renay's eyes adjust to see a body lying nearby. It's a large man with dark skin face down on the ground with snow-dusted around his frozen limp form.

Renay grabs Trevor and holds him, rocking him gently, trying to keep him warm. The cold causes her teeth to chatter and she knows if they don't get to someplace warm soon, they'll both freeze to death.

She looks up at the trail and sees a car parked a few hundred feet from a main road.

Hugging Trevor close to her, she gets to her feet, feeling him shiver. Another body is between them and the car and Renay walks by it close enough to see the torn wreckage of Wanda Burns.

Renay shields Trevor's eyes from the carnage and keeps walking. Near the car, a man's body is half hanging from the passenger side, gripping a gun in his hand with his frozen fingers attached to the trigger.

Renay goes to the other side of the car and puts Trevor in the back, then she goes to the passenger side and drags Carl Burns' frozen body out onto the ground.

Once he's out of the car, she gets behind the wheel and sees the keys are still there.

She starts the car and turns the heater to full blast.

Renay notices the gas guage is showing almost empty and she has no idea where she is, so takes her phone from her pocket. No service, of course. Renay does the only thing she can and activates the SOS feature in hopes someone gets the distress call before she and Trevor freeze to death out here.

Trevor screams and Renay instinctively reaches around to place an arm between her son and whatever threat he's perceived. To her astonishment, she sees Timmy, the child from the house, sitting on the opposite side. Black eyes stare intently at her son and a dark tongue lulls from a wide mouth crusted with blood and sharp, black teeth. It juts in and out like he's salivating for his next meal.

"Trevor! Open the door and get out of the car," Renay barks.

Timmy produces a scratchy voice like an old speaker that only half works. "Play. Please."

Trevor fiddles with the door but can't seem to get it open. Renay opens her door and jumps from the car as Timmy inches closer to Trevor. She pulls on the back door and her hand slips, causing her to fall forward and slip in the snow beneath her feet. Trevor wails inside and Renay grabs the side of the car and hoists herself to her feet, then pops the door open and reaches inside, wrapping her arms around her son, and pulling him out of the car. Timmy rolls out after him, clawing at the air with his sharp fingernails.

Renay directs her son to the open front door of the car, "Trevor, get in!"

Trevor does so and Renay steps back as Timmy follows her, falling into the snow.

She doesn't wait for him to regain his footing, only slams the back door shut, then jumps in the driver's side seat, closing the door behind her. She lets out the breath she's holding in, producing a long exhalation. Her hands tremble on the steering wheel as she stares forward into a grove of trees ahead of the vehicle. Renay turns to Trevor, noticing him shaking with wide eyes full of fear.

"Are you alright?" Renay asks.

He nods and sits back in the seat.

Suddenly, they hear a thump against the front windshield, and both let out a scream, as Timmy is there, staring them down, his fingers scraping the outside glass, making a sound like that of a chalkboard screeching.

His voice is muffled from outside, but he says the same as before. "Play. Please."

"Go away," Renay screams and hits the middle of the steering wheel. The horn blares and Timmy jumps, rolls off the hood of the car, and bounds into the woods near the edge of the river.

Renay's heart is thumping, beating like a runaway train. Her breath is uneven and coming in quick bursts while she tries to maintain some semblance of order in her psyche. She reaches for Trevor and pulls him close. The two hold each other tight.

"Mommy?" her son says. "I love you."

Renay squeezes him tighter and kisses the top of his head. "I love you too, baby."

Wind blows against the car, but they hear little other than the rumble of the vehicle's engine keeping them warm.

Thirty-One
Forensics

When the local PD arrives, they find a woman and a child in a car. They report she is Renay Reinhardt, and she's identified the boy as her missing son. Three dead bodies are reported as well. Two are the suspects the police are looking for.

Soon, detectives are on the scene as well as forensics. Renay and her son are taken to Portsmouth, Ohio to a local hospital to be checked out while the police perform an investigation of the grounds in Kentucky.

When the detectives arrive, they see a river, swollen and angry flowing close by, making its presence known by sight and sound near a field of frozen grass. The whole area is dead and uninviting. The perfect place to find all the carnage presented to them.

Detective Christina Fertig walks with Detective Ben Young by a Chevy Tahoe with the name of a funeral home on the side. A couple of people are loading the dead onto it for transport. The forensics team is already here, and Christina sees a man taking samples of the soil where the bodies were lying only moments ago.

Ben excuses himself to talk to a sheriff's deputy and State Policeman. Christina nods to him and heads over to where the forensics guy is crouching on the ground.

"Hey," she says to the man, "Detective Christina Fertig, of Columbus PD."

"Oh, how are you this morning, Detective," he says, "Joseph Murnane, but everyone calls me, Joey."

"So, from what you've seen, can you speculate on the cause of death?"

Joey shakes his head, "Looks like some kind of animal attack, but a weird one I don't think I've ever seen before."

"How so?" Christina asks.

"Well, the bite marks look like a wolf, but also a shark. Maybe somewhere in between. Like I said, weird."

"Also, there's the artifacts we found."

"Artifacts? What do you mean?"

"Over here," Joey motions for her to follow.

Christina walks with the young man to what appears to be a grave marker. It has words of some kind on it, but she can't read them. It's like they are written in a foreign language. "These are gravestones, right?"

Joey nods. "Yeah, I'm a bit of a history buff so I call them artifacts."

Christina ignores this and studies the gravestone instead, "What's it say?" she asks.

"It's in German, *Der Spiegel meiner Seele*, or The Mirror to my Soul. I suppose by the apparent age of the stone, this place had a lot of German immigrants at one time. It's not uncommon to see these off to themselves sometimes. If you look to the side over here, you'll see an old stone foundation.

Apparently, an old house sat there at one time or another."

"What does it have to do with the case?" Christina asks.

"Nothing really except we found one of the bodies right here next to the area. The Albanian guy. Oddly, he didn't have bite marks on him, but a hole burned through his middle."

She looks at Joey strangely. "Excuse me, did you say burned through him? What would cause such a thing?"

"I'm not exactly sure, but I would think the autopsy will reveal something. As far as the rest, I plan to go over to the county courthouse and the local library and see what I can find out about this house and graveyard. Maybe something to help the case. I might find a connection to why the bodies were here anyway. It's a long shot but you never know. I'll have a full report once the autopsy comes back."

"Okay, thank you, Joey. In the meantime, we'll question the victims and see if we can get any more. At least the abducted child is safe and with his mother."

"You know, if I didn't know any better, I'd think this is the work of a cryptid."

Christina scrunches her nose, "A what?"

"Oh, well, I run a podcast in my spare time and that's what we discuss on there, cryptids, or monsters of folklore, that kind of thing. This setup has all the hallmarks of a changeling or maybe Bag Man, even Krampus. We are close to Christmas, you know."

Christina shakes her head. "What are you talking about? Those are fairy tales."

"Yes, but they all have a connection to things in the real world. Fairy lore goes way back, thousands of years possibly and the others are creations of old Europe and Latin America, but they may have different names there. The thing is, they all have similar origins."

"I'm not following, Joey."

"We know this area dates back a way and there were immigrants here who probably believed in a lot of the things I mentioned.

The Ohio River Valley is full of cryptid sightings, The Moth man, The Goat Man, even Dog Men, and lizard people. It may not be a stretch to assume some of the lore could be connected to this case. Especially, if someone or a group of people, wanted to make it look that way."

"So, I'm to assume this is the work of a fairy tale? That is not a solid case, in fact, it would make it a cold case if there's no more substantial evidence. I'll stick with the autopsy if you don't mind."

"Of course, I'll get my findings to the medical examiner right away," Joey says and starts to turn away. "Hey, if you're ever interested, the name of my podcast is, The Cryptid Files. Listen to it wherever you download your podcasts."

Christina smiles. "Sure thing."

Joey goes on up the trail to the area where the other victims lay and Christina walks back to her waiting car where Ben is standing, shaking his head. "You finding the same dead ends I am?"

"Yeah, the whole thing makes no sense at all. Typically, an abduction means someone wants to extort money or it's a custody case. This is neither. Why would they bring the kid out here, and maybe his mother? She didn't drive here. We know that much anyway. She was found in the perp's car," Christina says.

"I don't know. She had plenty of time to get here after her son was taken and she ducked out of the hospital last night. I can see some suspicious behavior there. Maybe she was in it with them?"

Christina shakes her head. "No, it doesn't make sense. Did her bank accounts show any unexpected money drops?"

"Nothing out of the ordinary, just her regular pay from the clinic she works for," Ben says.

"Then why? Why go to all the trouble of staging an abduction and there is no money involved? I mean, there is the missing foster child. I wonder what she had to do with this?"

"There's something. We have a report from a neighbor of the Burns'. They said the girl was carried from the house yesterday afternoon over the shoulder of the big guy we found down by the grave markers. So, we know the abductors had her as well, but we've found no body. My guess is it'll show up downriver somewhere in the Spring when the water recedes."

"Maybe there's something here we're not accounting for, Ben? Is there evidence of another car? One that dropped Renay off before everything went down?"

"Nope, nothing but the tires of the abductors' vehicle and the cops who pulled in first on the scene."

"Well, I suppose we still have to question, Renay. I'm hoping she'll give us something to go on or at least a clue or two to figure this all out. Where is she?" Christina asks.

"In the hospital with her son, being checked out. She should be back at the precinct when we get to Portsmouth. We can question her then," Ben says.

Christina nods. "Let's head that way. I don't want to stay out in this cold any longer than I have to."

"Yeah, by the look of the sky, a good snowstorm may be brewing."

They both get in their cars and leave. Soon, the forensics team wraps up as well, leaving the field outside of Salt Flat as a barren and distant memory as it had been for many years.

The wind picks up and blows cold across the frozen ground and snow begins to fall across the grave markers and the field of dead grass. All will be covered in a few hours, and no one will notice the sound of small children calling out over the wind.

Thirty-Two
Reflection

The snow piles outside of the window, falling in large chunks, and blowing into the porch of Maddy Reinhardt's house. Renay watches her mom with Trevor, enjoying the spectacle through the fascination of her grandson's eyes as he sits beside her staring out the window.

Lights from the tree flash reflections of red, yellow, and white on the dark glass. Renay wonders if the brightness hurts her mom's head a little. If it does, she seems to ignore it for the sake of her grandson. The place on her head is healing slowly but after what happened, Renay doubts she'll ever be fully back to normal.

Renay's scar has calmed, no longer the red, angry welts that tormented her before. It began fading once they left the field. She supposed they all had healed in one way or another.

"Wow, Grandma, it's a blizzard outside," Trevor says.

"I don't think it's quite that level, but it is picking up. Santa should have no problem landing his sleigh tonight," Maddy says and hugs Trevor. "Better be getting to bed soon."

Trevor scrunches his face and makes his way to his mother who is sitting by the fireplace. The open gas log glows red with yellow flames behind it, giving out ample warmth. Renay turns away from her computer tablet to acknowledge him, extending her arms. He hops into her lap and puts his arms around her neck.

Renay nuzzles her head against his and squeezes him back. She stares at the tree close by with a few presents underneath—Trevor's would go under later, of course—and smiles. It was good to be here, warm and with the ones you loved. "You ready for tomorrow, big guy?"

He nods and tilts his head toward her, "Yes, I can't wait to see what Santa gets me. I have a present for you, too. Grandma helped me, it's a secret." He smiles widely. "A necklace."

Renay shakes her head. "Well, I'll make sure to act surprised."

"Mommy? Are you okay?"

"What do you mean?"

"I mean, do you still think about what happened to us in the field?"

Renay is shocked by this as she and Trevor are both going to therapy to alleviate some of the trauma they'd been through. But the therapist did say to talk things out when they came up. "I'm trying to put it behind us, but I still think about it. What about you?"

Trevor closes one eye and looks away, his face scrunches and then straightens. "I think a lot about that little boy and how weird he looked. I even dream about him and the shadow thing sometimes and it scares me."

Renay squeezes him tighter, "You know, if you ever have a nightmare, you can wake me up to talk about it, right?"

He nods and worry falls over his face. "What do you think happened to him? The little boy?"

She thinks about this but doesn't want to because she's had similar anxiety and would like to forget the whole thing. Renay wonders sometimes if she'll hear the tapping from the mirror again and wake to see him or the creature in there. It's something she would prefer to forget. "I hope he went far away and won't ever return."

"Is he bad?"

"I don't know, Trevor, maybe. But he was good at one time before he became what he did, but we'll never know. I want to make sure you're safe. I love you very much and I'll always be here for you. Now, better get up to bed."

"Okay, but don't forget to put out cookies for Santa and corn for the reindeer."

"Absolutely, we can't have the man with the presents hungry, can we?"

Trevor hops off her lap and goes to his waiting grandma. She takes his hand, and they disappear up the stairs. Renay reaches for her tablet and continues reading the article she had pulled up.

Missing Boy Found with Mother, is the headline and she knows what it says even before getting to the body of the article, but she reads it anyway.

A missing child was found on the outskirts of Salt Flat last week with his mother. The car they were found in belonged to the kidnappers, Carl and Wanda Burns. Another was named in the abduction as well. An Albanian man by the name of Bresnik Abrashi.

It's not clear how all were connected in the abduction, but it is believed Carl Burns and Abrashi had known each other for quite some time. All were found dead at the scene, Carl and Wanda Burns with bite marks indicating an animal attack and Abrashi with burns to his midsection.

The mother of the missing boy, Renay Reinhardt had no idea how the kidnappers were killed and only found them after she retrieved her son. She guessed it happened while the abductors were near the forest. She said something was there in the trees and she and Trevor, the missing boy, hid inside the car until it left.

Police found blood on the passenger side of the car, identified as belonging to Carl Burns. Renay Reinhardt reported seeing it and Burns' body hanging from the vehicle when she and Trevor arrived.

Another child was missing as well, Jessica Burns, the foster child of Carl and Wanda.

Neighbors reported seeing her being taken to the car from the Burns' house the night of the abduction. She remains unaccounted for.

Renay yawns and lays the tablet to the side, then turns out the lamp light. The snow outside is coming down fast and frost dusts the corners of the window as she reflects. So many things have happened she'll never forget, namely the girl she had to leave behind in that upside-down world. She wishes Jessica was here, right beside her, enjoying the peaceful evening, but is aware she'll always carry her in her heart.

Renay stares at the tree and watches the lights blink in and out in the darkened room.

Crouching in front of it, she sees her reflection in one of the ornaments. Renay stares for a moment, adjusting her eyes to the light around it, and notices another image beside her, standing to the side. Her heart skips a beat, and she turns but no one is there.

She stares at the ornament again, seeing only her image reflected back at her and sighs. "I know you're there and I'll see you again someday," she says to the empty room.

The skin around Renay's stomach burns suddenly and she places her hand there and smiles.

Thirty-Three
Epilogue

"Welcome to the Cryptid Files, the podcast where we delve into the mysterious sightings of those strange creatures everyone is talking about but only a few have seen. I'm your host Joseph Murnane and do we have a show for you."

Joey nods to the guest he has on the split screen.

"Today I'm joined by Rachel Madding to discuss the sightings of the Frog Man, residing around the Cincinnati area. But before we get into that, I want to talk about a more recent affair," Joey says, adjusting his headset. "As many of you know, I'm a forensics investigator for the Portsmouth Police Department, but also freelance for others who need me. Anyway, I worked on the case many have seen on the news lately. The kidnapped child, Trevor Reinhardt, from Columbus, Ohio. While I can't get into the specifics of the case as parts of it are still under investigation, I can tell you I saw things in that field to make me feel Cryptids were at work there," Joey says, smiling, then continues. "The mother of the stolen child reported seeing a boy near the car they were found in. She said he appeared rabid like a wild animal and attacked her and her son before she was able to get him out of the car. Now, we know a crazy kid is nothing, but what piqued my interest was what she said about his eyes. They were black as night with no distinct color to them," Joey says, pausing to take a drink of water before continuing on.

"So many of the Cryptids we report on this show have a similar appearance to the alien sightings with the large heads and black eyes. So, this makes me think we have a new one running around and I'm sure there will be sightings at some point. We'll be sure to follow up if we hear anything. Now, let's get back to that very familiar Cryptid, The Frog Man."

Joey switches to his guest and the podcast goes on to all of his two hundred subscribed members.

◆○◆

Somewhere near the Ohio River bank, close to a town called Salt Flat in Kentucky, a child roams around the gravestones in a field. Its teeth are blood-stained and it seems to have an insatiable urge for meat.

Many of the local farmers have reported losses of chickens and a few calves and goats. Hunters also report sightings and wildlife eaten, only the bloody remains left strewn across the ground—the attacks more vicious than any wildcat, coyote, or wolf could accomplish.

Strange burn marks were found on the animals as well; the skin charred around the edges of the ripped open carcasses. All mauled by a creature they have no way of explaining.

Where it came from, nobody knows, but this ghoulish figure has already captured the attention of the pseudo-scientific com-

munity. A thing more supernatural than real, but that's a story for
another time.

The End

Acknowledgements

I would like to acknowledge some of the great people who made this book possible. First off the readers and reviewers of my Advanced Readers Copy group. The early reviews for this book have been wonderful and I greatly appreciate your input. Especially, Joan S. Smith, Alexandra Nisneru, Jyl Glenn, Sophie Griffiths, Liz hargrove, Chiara Cooper, and Theresa Hayden.

My cover artist, Ruth Anna Evans for making my vision a reality with the stunning cover of this book. Dagan Boyd for the incredible interior images seen on the print version of the book.

To Ben Young, an author and someone I'm honored to call a friend. He was one of the earliest readers of the book you have now, along with Amber Applegate and Ruthann Jagge. The insight they all gave me helped shape the final reading of this book.

To my editor, Monique Snyman, whose vision of what this book could be helped guide me in a new direction.

To my wife, Mikel Stone, who as an Occupational Therapist helped me with some of the more technical aspects of the book. I haven't worked in pediatrics in years and her knowledge was a fantastic refresher course.

To Books of Horror, my tribe of weirdos and horror fans. So many people there who relate to the horror genre and a place I frequent often. If you love horror and you want a place to talk about your latest horror read, then you owe it to youself to be there. RJ Roles, Tiffany Koplin, Lance Dale, Heather Larson, Rhonda Lynn Bobbitt, and so many more keep the wheels rolling over there. Thank you all.

A special shoutout to Lauren Young and Ben Young. This dynamic duo help so many authors, known and just getting started, to find a voice. Their live interviews on Books of Horror are a treat to watch. Check them out as soon as you can.

Finally, to my little fan group on Facebook, Edmund's Stoners, who love to get stoned on horror. I started this little group after Books and Brews event in August 2024 and it has been steadily growing ever since. Thanks to the top contributors, Mary Loomer Trujillo, Dennis Sara Sweeney, Christina L. Fertig, Mari Pittelman, Angel Ramon, Shannon O'Neill, Kathy Barrett, Dawn Schock, Lauren Young, Joeseph Murnane Polinger, and Erica Wetzel-Fields. Also to Ben Young and Mikel Stone for their roles as administrators.

Thanks to everyone and I hope you enjoyed this book. Make sure to leave a review if you are so inclined.

About the Author

Edmund Stone is a writer of horror and suspense, and a part time boat captain. He resides in a home along the Ohio River with his wife, four dogs, and a group of mischievous cats. He is the author of several books and short story collections. He has many short stories residing in various anthologies as well. His books can be found on Amazon, Barnes and Noble, independent bookstores, and at Crystal Lake Publishing.

Find him at edmudstonehorror.com or his Linktree page: https://lintr.ee/edmundstoneauthor

While on edmundstonehorror.com be sure to sign up for my newsletter to get a free story and all the latest information on new releases from Edmund Stone Author.

The End?

Not if you want to dive into more of Crystal Lake Publishing's Tales from the Darkest Depths!

Check out our amazing website and online store or download out latest catalog here.
https://geni.us/CLPCatalog

We have great new projects and content on the website to dive into, as well as a newsletter, behind the scenes options, social media platforms, our own dark fiction shared-world series and our very own webstore. Our webstore even has categories specifically for KU books, non-fiction, anthologies, and of course more novels and novellas.

Readers…

Thank you for reading *Soul Mirror*. We hope you enjoyed this novel. If you have a moment, please review *Soul Mirror* at the store where you bought it.

Help other readers by telling them why you enjoyed this book. No need to write an in-depth discussion. Even a single sentence will be greatly appreciated. Reviews go a long way to helping a book sell, and is great for an author's career. It'll also help us to continue publishing quality books.

Thank you again for taking the time to journey with Crystal Lake Publishing.

Visit our Linktree page for a list of our social media platforms.
https://linktr.ee/CrystalLakePublishing

Follow us on Amazon:

Mission Statement

Since its founding in August 2012, Crystal Lake has quickly become one of the world's leading publishers of Dark Fiction and Horror books. In 2023, Crystal Lake officially transitioned into an entertainment company, joining several other divisions, genres, and imprints, including Torrid Waters, Crystal Lake Comics, Crystal Lake Games, Crystal Lake Kids, and many more.

While we strive to present only the highest quality fiction and entertainment, we also endeavour to support authors along their writing journey. We offer our time and experience in non-fiction projects, as well as author mentoring and services, at competitive prices.

With several Bram Stoker Award wins and many other wins and nominations (including the HWA's Specialty Press Award), Crystal Lake Publishing puts integrity, honor, and respect at the forefront of our publishing operations.

We strive for each book and outreach program we spearhead to not only entertain and touch or comment on issues that affect our readers, but also to strengthen and support the Dark Fiction field and its authors.

Not only do we find and publish authors we believe are destined for greatness, but we strive to work with men and women who endeavour to be decent human beings who care more for others than themselves, while still being hard working, driven, and passionate artists and storytellers.

Crystal Lake Publishing is and will always be a beacon of what passion and dedication, combined with overwhelming teamwork and respect, can accomplish. We endeavour to know each and every one of our readers, while building personal relationships with our authors, reviewers, bloggers, podcasters, bookstores, and libraries.

We will be as trustworthy, forthright, and transparent as any business can be, while also keeping most of the headaches away from our authors, since it's our job to solve the problems so they can stay in a creative mind. Which of course also means paying our authors.

We do not just publish books, we present to you worlds within your world, doors within your mind, from talented authors who sacrifice so much for a moment of your time.

There are some amazing small presses out there, and through collaboration and open forums we will continue to support other presses in the goal of helping authors and showing the world what quality small presses are capable of accomplishing. No one wins when a small press goes down, so we will always be there to support hardworking, legitimate presses and their authors. We don't see Crystal Lake as the best press out there, but we will always strive to be the best, strive to be the most interactive and grateful, and even blessed press around. No matter what happens over time, we will also take our mission very seriously while appreciating where we are and enjoying the journey.

What do we offer our authors that they can't do for themselves through self-publishing?

We are big supporters of self-publishing (especially hybrid publishing), if done with care, patience, and planning. However, not every author has the time or inclination to do market research, advertise, and set up book launch strategies. Although a lot of authors are successful in doing it all, strong small presses will always be there for the authors who just want to do what they do best: write.

What we offer is experience, industry knowledge, contacts and trust built up over years. And due to our strong brand and trusting fanbase, every Crystal Lake Publishing book comes with weight of respect. In time our fans begin to trust our judgment and will try a new author purely based on our support of said author.

With each launch we strive to fine-tune our approach, learn from our mistakes, and increase our reach. We continue to assure our authors that we're here for them and that we'll carry the weight of the launch and dealing with third parties while they focus on their strengths—be it writing, interviews, blogs, signings, etc.

We also offer several mentoring packages to authors that include knowledge and skills they can use in both traditional and self-publishing endeavours.

We look forward to launching many new careers.

This is what we believe in. What we stand for. This will be our legacy.

**Welcome to Crystal Lake Publishing—
Where Stories Come Alive!**

THANK YOU FOR PURCHASING THIS BOOK